## The Outsider

Albert Camus was born in Algeria in 1913. He studied philosophy at the University of Algiers, then became a journalist, as well as organising the Theatre de l'équipe, a young avant-garde dramatic group. His early essays were collected in *L'Envers et l'endroit* (The Wrong Side and the Right Side) and *Noces* (Nuptials). As a young man, he went to Paris, where he worked on the newspaper *Paris Soir* before returning to Algiers. His play, *Caligula*, appeared in 1939, while his first two important books, *L'Etranger* (The Outsider) and the philosophical essays collected in *Le Mythe de Sisyphe* (The Myth of Sisyphus), were published when he returned to Paris. After the occupation of France by the Germans in 1940, Camus became one of the intellectual leaders of the Resistance movement. He edited and contributed to the underground newspaper *Combat*, which he had helped to found. After the war, he devoted himself to writing and established an international reputation with such books as *La Peste* (The Plague) (1947), *Les Justes* (The Just) (1949) and *La Chute* (The Fall) (1956). During the late 1950s, Camus renewed his active interest in the theatre, writing and directing stage adaptations of William Faulkner's *Requiem for a Nun* and Dostoyevsky's *The Possessed*. He was awarded the Nobel Prize for Literature in 1957. Camus was killed in a road accident in 1960. His last novel, *Le Premier Homme* (The First Man), unfinished at the time of his death, appeared for the first time in 1994. An instant bestseller, the book received widespread critical acclaim, and has been translated and published in over thirty countries. Much of Camus's work is available in Penguin.

Sandra Smith was born in New York and studied at NYU, the Sorbonne and Cambridge University. She won the French American Foundation Florence Gould Foundation Translation Prize, as well as the PEN Book-of-the-Month Club Translation Prize. She is a Fellow of Robinson College, Cambridge, where she teaches French language and literature.

# ALBERT CAMUS

## *The Outsider*

*Translated by* SANDRA SMITH

PENGUIN BOOKS

PENGUIN CLASSICS

Published by the Penguin Group
Penguin Books Ltd, 80 Strand, London WC2R 0RL, England
Penguin Group (USA) Inc., 375 Hudson Street, New York, New York 10014, USA
Penguin Group (Canada), 90 Eglinton Avenue East, Suite 700, Toronto, Ontario, Canada M4P 2Y3
(a division of Pearson Penguin Canada Inc.)
Penguin Ireland, 25 St Stephen's Green, Dublin 2, Ireland (a division of Penguin Books Ltd)
Penguin Group (Australia), 707 Collins Street, Melbourne, Victoria 3008, Australia
(a division of Pearson Australia Group Pty Ltd)
Penguin Books India Pvt Ltd, 11 Community Centre, Panchsheel Park, New Delhi – 110 017, India
Penguin Group (NZ), 67 Apollo Drive, Rosedale, Auckland 0632, New Zealand
(a division of Pearson New Zealand Ltd)
Penguin Books (South Africa) (Pty) Ltd, Block D, Rosebank Office Park,
181 Jan Smuts Avenue, Parktown North, Gauteng 2193, South Africa

Penguin Books Ltd, Registered Offices: 80 Strand, London WC2R 0RL, England

www.penguin.com

First published in French as *L'Étranger* by Librairie Gallimard 1942
This translation first published in Penguin Classics 2012
This edition published in Penguin Classics 2013

016

Copyright 1942 Albert Camus
Translation and Note on the Text © Sandra Smith, 2012
All rights reserved

The moral rights of the author and the translator have been asserted

Set in 11.25/13pt Minion Regular
Typeset by Jouve (UK), Milton Keynes
Printed in Great Britain by Clays Ltd, Elcograf S.p.A.

ISBN: 978-0-141-19806-4

www.greenpenguin.co.uk

Penguin Books is committed to a sustainable
future for our business, our readers and our planet.
This book is made from Forest Stewardship
Council™ certified paper.

## Translator's Note

Readers may wonder why a new translation of *The Outsider* is necessary. Primarily, it is essential to create new versions of classic works in another language because language constantly evolves. The original text is immutable yet translations should be written in a style that is accessible to the modern reader while conveying the spirit of the foreign text. Idiomatic speech in particular needs to be rendered in a way that feels true to the original without sounding dated. This is especially important in *The Outsider*, as Camus writes in the first person. For this reason, I listened to a recording of Camus's own reading of the novel on French radio in 1954, to try to replicate the nuances of his rendition.

Another demanding aspect of translation arises from the fact that a single word in another language often has multiple connotations that are difficult to encapsulate. A translator is therefore forced to make linguistic choices based on a subjective interpretation of the work. The title of the novel itself offers the perfect example of this phenomenon. In French, *étranger* can be translated as 'outsider', 'stranger' or 'foreigner'. Our protagonist, Meursault, is all three, and the concept of an outsider encapsulates all these possible meanings:

Meursault is a stranger to himself, an outsider to society and a foreigner because he is a Frenchman in Algeria.

In some cases, I have used more than one word in English to translate a specific term in French so as not to detract from the richness of Camus's implications or its multiplicity of meaning. In one of the most important scenes of the novel, for instance, Camus uses the metaphor of knocking on the door of *malheur*. In French, this single word has a wealth of associations: destiny, disaster, unhappiness, misfortune, accident, ordeal, mishap, tragedy. To convey this density of interpretation, I chose to expand the phrase, translating it as 'the fatal door of destiny'.

There are two additional interpretations in the existing English-language versions that, in my view, do not adequately reflect the original text. The first is the translation of *maman* as 'Mother'. 'Mother' is quite formal and fails to convey the intimacy implied in French by *maman*, yet the British equivalent, 'Mummy', and the American 'Mommy' would sound too juvenile. I chose to use 'Mother' in the famous first line of the book, to reflect Meursault's shock at receiving the telegram that announces her death in such a terse, formal manner. 'Mama' is a better translation elsewhere, indicating a closer, more affectionate relationship, despite the protagonist's apparent oddness. This point is poignantly demonstrated at the end of the novel when Meursault states that he understands that his mother had been happy, so no one has the right to cry over her. The contrast between Meursault's behaviour towards his mother and his use of the word *maman* when referring to her is a paradox that adds considerably to the feeling of tension and dislocation in the novel.

The second instance appears at the very end of the book, where Camus writes: '*je m'ouvrais pour la première fois à la tendre indifférence du monde*' ('I opened myself for the first time to the tender indifference of the world'). For some reason, *tendre* is rendered as 'benign' in most previous translations, a choice that fails to capture the paradoxical nuance of 'tender'. As Camus once wrote in his notebooks: '*Si tu veux être philosophe, écris des romans*' ('If you want to be a philosopher, write novels'). This one word at the most critical point in the novel radically changes the entire philosophical perspective of the work.

An additional challenge I faced when translating this work was how to convey the allusions to religion in the novel. Camus famously remarked that Meursault was 'the only Christ we deserve'. He went on to explain that he meant no 'blasphemy' by this; he was simply pointing out that his protagonist was prepared to die rather than lie, or 'play the game'.

There are many key scenes in the second part of the novel that deal with Christianity and its ethical link to the judicial system. One of the most important allusions to religion, however, is in the final line of the novel. Camus has his protagonist say: '*Pour que tout soit consommé*', an echo of the last words of Jesus on the Cross: '*Tout est consommé.*' As the translation of this sentence in the King James Bible is 'It is finished', I chose to render this extremely significant phrase as 'So that it might be finished', retaining the formal language of the Bible to help guide the reader towards the religious implications of the words.

Throughout the translation, I have retained the direct, staccato style that Camus uses to reflect Meursault's persona. The most lyrical passages in the novel are the striking descriptions of nature, in particular the sun and sea imagery, and I have followed Camus's approach in these sections.

Translating this important work has been a great honour and I am grateful to Penguin for this opportunity. I would also like to thank the following people for their help and support: my husband Peter, my son Harrison, Dr Paul Micio, Anne Garvey, Dr Jacques Beauroy, Lucas Demurger and my colleagues at Robinson College, Cambridge.

Sandra Smith
May 2012

*Part One*

# 1

My mother died today. Or maybe yesterday, I don't know. I received a telegram from the old people's home: 'Mother deceased. Funeral tomorrow. Very sincerely yours.' That doesn't mean anything. It might have been yesterday.

The old people's home is in Marengo, eighty kilometres from Algiers. I'll get the bus at two o'clock and arrive in the afternoon. That way I can be at the wake and come home tomorrow night. I asked my boss for two days off and he couldn't say no given the circumstances. But he didn't seem happy about it. I even said: 'It's not my fault.' He didn't reply. Then I thought I shouldn't have said that. Although I had nothing to apologize for. He was the one who should have been offering me his condolences. But he'll no doubt say something the day after tomorrow when he sees me dressed in black. For now, it's still a little as if Mama hadn't died. After the funeral, however, it will be over and done with, a matter that is officially closed.

I got the bus at two o'clock. It was very hot. I ate at Céleste's restaurant as I always do. Everyone felt very sorry for me, and Céleste said: 'You only have one mother.' When I got up to leave, they walked me to the door. I felt a little strange because I had to go up to Emmanuel's place to borrow a black tie and armband. He lost his uncle a few months ago.

I had to run to catch the bus. Rushing around, running like that, plus the bumpy ride, the smell of petrol, the sun's glare reflecting off the road, all that must have been why I felt so drowsy. I slept for nearly the whole journey. When I woke up, I was leaning against a soldier who smiled at me and asked if I had come a long way. I said 'Yes' so I wouldn't have to talk any more.

The old people's home is two kilometres from the village. I walked. I wanted to see Mama right away. But the caretaker told me I had to meet the director first. He was busy, so I had to wait a while. The caretaker talked the whole time and then I saw the director; he showed me into his office. He was a short, elderly man who wore the Legion of Honour. He looked at me with his pale blue eyes. Then he shook my hand, but he held on to it for so long that I didn't quite know how to pull it away. He looked at some papers, then said: 'Madame Meursault came to us three years ago. You were the only one who could support her financially.' I thought he was reproaching me for something and started to explain. But he stopped me: 'You have no reason to justify yourself, my dear boy. I've read your mother's file. You weren't able to look after all her needs. She required a nurse. You earn a very modest living. And to tell the truth, she was happier here with us.' I said: 'Yes, Monsieur.' 'She had friends here, you know,' he added, 'people of her own age. She could share her interests from the past with them. You're young and she was probably bored when she was living with you.'

It was true. When we lived together, Mama spent all her time silently watching me come and go. The first few days she was at the old people's home, she often cried. But that was because her routine had changed. After a few months, she would have cried if she'd been taken out of the home. For the same reason. That was partly why I hadn't gone to visit her very often during the past year. And also because it took up my whole Sunday – not to mention the time and effort to buy the ticket, get the bus and travel for two hours each way.

The director was talking to me again but I was barely listening. Then he said: 'I assume you would like to see your mother.' I stood up without saying anything and followed him out the door. On the staircase, he explained: 'We put her in our little mortuary so we didn't upset the others. Every time one of our residents dies, they feel anxious for two or three days. And that makes it difficult for us to do our job.' We walked through a courtyard where there were a lot of old people chatting in little groups. They stopped talking as we walked by. Once we had passed, their conversations started up again; they sounded like parakeets squawking in the distance. When we reached the door of a small building, the director stopped: 'I'll leave you here, Monsieur Meursault. I'll be in my office if you need anything. The funeral was set for ten o'clock tomorrow morning so you could attend the wake of your dearly departed. One more thing: your mother, it seems, often told her companions that she wished to have a religious burial. I have taken the liberty of arranging everything. But I wanted to let you know.' I thanked him. While not actually an atheist, Mama had never once in her life given a thought to religion.

I went inside. The room was very bright, whitewashed, with a glass roof. There were chairs and trestles in the shape of an X. In the centre of the room, two of them supported the coffin; the lid was closed. All you could see were its shiny metal screws, barely secured, sticking out from the stained walnut planks. Near the coffin there was an Arab nurse in a white smock, wearing a brightly coloured scarf over her head.

At that moment, the caretaker came in behind me. He must have been running, he stammered a little: 'We closed the casket, so I have to unscrew the lid for you to see her.' He started walking towards the coffin but I stopped him. 'You don't want to?' he asked. I replied: 'No.' He stopped and I was uncomfortable because I felt I shouldn't have said that. After a moment, he looked at me and asked: 'Why?' but without sounding reproachful, just as if he were simply asking a question. I said: 'I don't know.' Then he twirled his white moustache through his fingers and, without looking at me, he said: 'I understand.' He had beautiful light blue eyes and a slightly ruddy complexion. He brought a chair over for me and then sat down himself a little behind me. The nurse stood up and headed for the exit. At that moment, the caretaker said: 'She has leprosy.' I didn't understand, so I looked up at the nurse and saw that she had a bandage around her head just below her eyes. It sat flat where her nose had been eaten away by the disease. All you could see was the whiteness of the bandage against her face.

After she left, the caretaker said: 'I'll leave you alone.' I don't know what gesture I made but he stood at the back of my chair and didn't move. His presence behind me made me feel uncomfortable. It was late afternoon; the room was bathed in a beautiful light. Two hornets buzzed around the window. I could feel myself getting sleepy. Without turning around, I asked the caretaker: 'Have you been here long?' He immediately replied: 'Five years' – as if he had been waiting, forever, for me to ask.

Then he talked for a long time. He would have been very surprised if anyone had told him he'd end up a caretaker in an old people's home in Marengo. He was sixty-four years old and from Paris. I interrupted him to ask: 'Ah, so you're not from around here?' Then I remembered that before taking me to the director's office, he had talked about Mama. He'd told me they would have to bury her very quickly because it was so hot in the open country, especially in these parts. Then he told me he used to live in Paris and found it difficult to forget it. In Paris, people stayed with the dead person for three, four days sometimes. Here there's no time for that, you've barely come to terms with what's happened when you have to rush out to follow the hearse. Then his wife said: 'Do be quiet, you shouldn't be telling the gentleman such things.' The old man blushed and apologized. 'It's all right,' I cut in, 'it's all right.' I agreed with what he said and found it interesting.

In the little mortuary, he told me he had no money at all when he first came to the home. Since he considered himself healthy, he had offered to take on the job of caretaker. I pointed out to him that when all was said and done, he was one of the residents. He said he wasn't. I had already been struck by the way he said 'they', 'the others' and, more rarely, 'the old people' when he spoke about the residents, some of whom were the same age as him. But naturally it was different. He was the caretaker and to a certain extent he had more privileges and some authority over them.

Then the nurse came in. Night had fallen quite suddenly.

Very quickly, the sky had grown heavy and darker above the glass roof. The caretaker switched on the lights and I was blinded by the sudden burst of brightness. He invited me to come to the dining hall to eat, but I wasn't hungry. He then offered to bring me a cup of milky coffee. I like coffee, so I said yes, and a moment later he came back carrying some on a tray. I drank it. Then I wanted a cigarette. But I hesitated because I didn't know if I should smoke in front of Mama. I thought about it: it was of no importance whatsoever. I offered the caretaker a cigarette and we both smoked.

'You know,' he said to me after a moment, 'your mother's friends are going to come to the wake as well. It's the custom here. I have to go and get some more chairs and coffee.' I asked him if he could switch off one of the lights. Their harsh reflection off the white walls was making me sleepy. He told me it wasn't possible. That's how the lights worked: it was all or nothing. I didn't pay much attention to him after that. He went out, came back, set up the chairs. He put some cups around a coffee pot on one of them. Then he sat down opposite me, on the other side of Mama. The nurse was also at the back, but turned away from me so that I couldn't see what she was doing. Judging by the way her arms were moving, though, I could tell she was knitting. It was cooler now; the coffee had warmed me up and the night air drifted in through the open door, bringing with it the sweet scent of flowers. I think I fell asleep for a while.

I was awakened by something brushing against me. My eyes had been closed and now the room seemed even more dazzling white. There wasn't a single shadow and every object, every angle, every curve stood out so sharply that it hurt my eyes. At that very moment, Mama's friends came in.

There were about ten of them in all and they silently slipped into the room beneath that blinding light. They sat down and not a single chair creaked. I looked at them as I had never looked at anyone before, taking in every detail of their faces and clothing. But I couldn't hear them, so I found it difficult to believe they were real. Almost all the women wore aprons tied tightly around their waists, which made their stomachs look even rounder. I had never noticed how old women could have such big stomachs. The men were almost all very thin and walked with a cane. What struck me most about their faces was that I couldn't see their eyes, just a faint, dull light in a nest of wrinkles. Once they had sat down, most of them looked at me and nodded as if they felt embarrassed; their lips looked sucked in because they had no teeth; I couldn't tell whether they were acknowledging me or if their mouths were just twitching. I think they were probably acknowledging me. It was just then that I noticed they were all sitting opposite me, around the caretaker, nodding their heads. For a split second, I had the ridiculous feeling that they were there to judge me.

Soon afterwards, one of the women started to cry. She was sitting in the second row, hidden by one of her friends, and I couldn't really see her. She cried softly, continually; I felt she would never stop. The others didn't seem to hear her. They were huddled in their chairs, sad and silent. They looked at the coffin or their canes or some other object in the room, seeing nothing else. The woman kept on crying. I was very surprised because I didn't know who she was. I wanted her to stop. But I didn't dare tell her. The caretaker leaned over and spoke to her but she just shook her head, mumbled something and carried on crying with the same

9

regular rhythm. Then the caretaker came over and sat down beside me. After a long time and without looking at me, he explained: 'She was very close to your mother. She says that she was her only friend here and that now she has no one.'

We sat like this for a long time. The woman's sighs and sobs grew fainter and fainter. She sniffled a lot. Finally, she fell silent. I wasn't sleepy any more but I was tired and my back ached. At that moment, it was the silence of all those people that was hard to bear. Every now and then, I heard a strange sound, but I couldn't make out what it was. In the end, I worked it out: some of the old people were sucking in their cheeks, making odd clicking noises. They were so engrossed in their thoughts that they didn't realize they were doing it. I even had the impression that this dead woman, stretched out in front of them, meant nothing to them. But now . . . I think I was wrong about that.

The caretaker served everyone coffee. I don't know what happened next. The night passed. I remember that I opened my eyes at one point and saw that some of the old people were asleep, huddled up against each other, except for one man who had his chin resting on his hands on top of his walking stick; he was staring at me as if he were waiting for me to wake up. Then I went back to sleep. I woke up because my back was hurting more. Dawn crept gradually in through the glass roof. A little while afterwards, one of the old people woke up and coughed a lot. He spat into a large chequered handkerchief and each time it sounded as if his cough was being wrenched from his body. He woke the others and the caretaker said it was time for them to go. Everyone stood up. This upsetting wake had turned their faces ashen. To my great astonishment, they each shook hands with me as they filed out – as if this night had sealed a bond of intimacy between us, even though we hadn't exchanged a single word.

I was tired. The caretaker took me to his room and I could freshen up a bit. I had another coffee; it was very good. By the time I went outside, day had fully dawned. Reddish streaks filled the sky high over the hills that separate Marengo from the sea. And the wind blowing from that direction carried with it the scent of salty air. It was going to be a beautiful day. It had been a long time since I'd gone to the countryside and I thought how nice it would be to go for a long walk, if it hadn't been for Mama.

But I stood waiting in the courtyard, beneath a plane tree. I breathed in the scent of the cool earth and didn't feel sleepy any more. I thought about my colleagues at work. They'd be getting up to go to the office about now; this was always the most difficult time of the day for me. I thought about that a little more, but then I was distracted by the sound of a bell ringing from somewhere inside the home. You could hear the hustle and bustle behind the windows, then everything quietened down. The sun had risen a bit higher in the sky; it was beginning to warm my feet. The caretaker crossed the courtyard and told me that the director wanted to see me. I went to his office. He had me sign several documents. I noticed he was dressed in black and wearing striped trousers. He picked up the phone and called out to me: 'The undertakers have just arrived. I'm going to ask them to close the coffin. Do you want to see your mother one last time before they do?' I said no. He spoke quietly into the phone and gave the order: 'Figeac, tell the men they can go ahead.'

Then he told me he would be coming to the funeral and I thanked him. He sat down behind his desk, crossing his short legs. He explained that he and I would be alone with the nurse on duty. In principle, the residents weren't permitted to go to funerals. He only allowed them to attend the wake. 'It's easier for them that way,' he said. But, in this particular case, he had given permission for an elderly friend of Mama's to walk behind the cortège: 'Thomas Pérez.' Then the director smiled. 'You see,' he told me, 'it's rather childish, but he and your mother were hardly ever apart. Here at the home, they were teased about it; people would say to Pérez: "She's your fiancée." Then he'd laugh. It made them happy. And it's true that Madame Meursault's death has upset him a great deal. I didn't see how I could refuse him permission. But on the doctor's advice, I didn't allow him to attend the wake last night.'

We sat in silence for a long time. The director stood up and looked out of his office window. At one point, he remarked: 'There's the parish priest from Marengo. He's early.' He explained to me that it would take at least three-quarters of an hour to walk to the church in the centre of the village. We went downstairs. The priest and two children who sang in the choir were standing in front of the building. One of them was holding a censer and the priest bent down to adjust its silver chain. When we arrived, the priest stood up. He called me 'my son' and said a few words to me. He went inside; I followed him.

I noticed right away that the screws on the coffin had been tightened and that there were four men in the room dressed in black. I heard the director tell me that the hearse was waiting out on the road and at the same time the priest started to pray. After that, everything happened very quickly. The men walked over to the coffin carrying a large cloth to cover it. The priest, the children from the choir who followed behind him, the director and I went outside. There was a woman I didn't know standing by the door. 'This is Monsieur Meursault,' said the director. I didn't catch the woman's name, but I realized she was a nurse who worked at the home. She nodded, with no smile on her long, bony face, then we all stepped aside to let the body pass. We followed the pall-bearers out of the home. The hearse was waiting in front of the door. Polished, shiny and oblong, it looked a little like a pencil case. Beside it stood the funeral director, a short man in a ridiculous outfit, and an old man who looked self-conscious. I realized this was Monsieur Pérez. He had on a light felt hat with a round top and a wide brim (he took it off as the coffin came through the door), a suit with trousers that hung down over his shoes and a black bowtie that looked too small for the large collar of his white shirt. His lips were trembling beneath a nose dotted with blackheads. Through his rather fine white hair you could see he had odd, misshapen ears that drooped down and whose blood-red colour was striking against his pallid face. The funeral director told us where to stand. The priest was at the front, followed by the hearse, and around it the four pall-bearers. Behind came the director of the home and me, and completing the funeral procession, the nurse and Monsieur Pérez.

The sky was already bathed in sunlight. It was beginning to weigh down heavily on the earth and the heat intensified with every passing minute. I don't know why we waited so long before setting off. I felt hot in my black clothes. The frail old man had put his hat back on but now took it off again. I turned slightly towards Pérez and looked at him while the director told me about him. He said that my mother and Monsieur Pérez often used to walk to the village together in the evening, accompanied by a nurse. I looked at the countryside all around me. When I saw the rows of cyprus trees leading into the hills high against the sky, and the green and reddish land, the houses dotted here and there, I understood how Mama must have felt. Out here in the country, evening must have offered a wistful moment of peace. But today the sun blazing down upon the shimmering landscape made it inhuman and depressing.

We started walking. That was when I noticed that Pérez was limping slightly. Gradually, the hearse picked up speed, and the old man started lagging behind. The hearse also passed one of the men who had been alongside it and he was now walking beside me. I was surprised at how quickly the sun had risen in the sky. I became conscious that for a long time the countryside had been buzzing with the hum of insects and the soft crackling of grass. Sweat ran down my face. Since I didn't have a hat, I fanned myself with my handkerchief. Then the man from the funeral home said something to me that I couldn't hear. He wiped his head with a handkerchief he was holding in his left hand, and pushed up the brim of his hat with the other. 'What did you say?' I asked. 'It's terribly hot,' he repeated, pointing to the sun. 'Yes,' I replied. A moment later, he asked: 'Is that your mother in the hearse?' I said 'Yes' again. 'Was she old?' I replied: 'Sort of', because I didn't know exactly how old she was. Then he stopped talking. I turned around and saw old Monsieur Pérez about fifty metres behind us. He was holding his hat out in front of him and trying to walk quickly; it flapped as he hurried. I also looked at the director. He walked with great dignity, every gesture measured and purposeful. A few beads of perspiration had formed on his forehead, but he didn't wipe them away.

It seemed as if the procession was moving more quickly now. All around me the landscape was still glaring, flooded in sunlight. The dazzling sky was unbearable. At one point, we walked over a section of road that had just been resurfaced. The sun had burned and blistered the tar. Our feet sank down into it, exposing its shimmering soft mass to the sun. Just visible above the hearse, the driver's hardened leather hat looked as if it had been moulded from the same black slime. I felt a bit lost standing between the blue and white of the sky and the relentless darkness of these other colours: the sticky black of the blistering tar, the dull black of the mourning clothes, the shiny black of the hearse. The sun, the smell of leather and dung clinging on to the wheels of the hearse, the smell of polish and incense, the exhaustion from not having slept all night – all these things stung my eyes and blurred my thoughts. I turned around again: Pérez looked very far away, fading in a cloudy haze of heat until I lost sight of him. I looked around for him and saw he had turned off the road and taken a path across a field. I also noticed that the road in front of me was curving. I realized that Pérez knew the area and was taking a short cut to catch up with us. By the time we came around the bend, he was beside us. Then we lost sight of him again. He took another country lane and did the same thing several times. All I could feel was the blood pounding against my temples.

Everything that happened next took place so quickly, so

efficiently, so effortlessly, that I no longer remember anything about it. Except for one thing: as we were entering the
village, the nurse spoke to me. She had an unusual voice
that seemed inconsistent with her face, a trembling, melo-
dious voice. 'If you walk too slowly,' she said, 'you risk getting
sunstroke. But if you go too quickly, you're sweating by the
time you reach the church and then you catch a chill.' She
was right. There was no escaping it. Certain moments from
that day have stayed with me: for instance, the look on
Pérez's face when he caught up with us for the last time
near the village. Great tears of fear and pain were flowing
down his cheeks. But because he had so many wrinkles,
they collected there. They formed little pools in the furrows
of his devastated face, covering it in a glistening film of
water. Then there was the church and the townspeople out
on the streets, the red geraniums on the graves in the cem-
etery, the moment when Pérez fainted (he looked like a
puppet collapsing to the ground when someone lets go of
the strings), the earth – the colour of blood – thrown over
Mama's coffin, the soft white roots mixed in with the dirt,
more people, more voices, the village, waiting in front of a
café, the relentless droning of the engine and my joy when,
at last, the bus pulled into the cluster of lights of Algiers and
I knew I could soon go to bed and sleep for twelve hours.

## 2

When I woke up, I understood why my boss hadn't seemed very happy when I asked for two days off: today is Saturday. I had more or less forgotten that, but realized it when I got up. My boss, quite naturally, must have thought that would mean I'd have four days off, including Sunday, which he probably wouldn't have liked. But then again, it's not my fault that Mama's funeral was yesterday instead of today, and I still would have had Saturday and Sunday off in any case. Of course, that doesn't mean I can't understand why my boss wasn't happy.

I had difficulty getting up because I was still tired from yesterday. While I was shaving, I wondered what I should do and I decided to go swimming. I took the tram to the public swimming pool near the port. I dived into one of the lanes. There were a lot of young people around. In the water, I saw Marie Cardona, a typist who used to work at my office and whom I'd found attractive at the time. It was mutual, I think. But she wasn't there for long so we didn't have time to do anything about it. I helped her climb on to a floating platform and my hand brushed against her breasts. I was still in the water; she'd already turned over on to her stomach and stretched out on the platform. She turned towards me. Her hair had fallen over her eyes and she was laughing.

I hoisted myself up next to her. It was warm and felt good, and, pretending it was a bit of a joke, I dropped my head back and let it rest on her stomach. She didn't say anything so I didn't move. I could see all of the sky above me, blue and golden. I could feel Marie's stomach under my neck, moving gently as she breathed. We stayed that way for a long time, half asleep. When the sun got too hot, she jumped into the water and I followed her. I caught up with her, put my arm around her waist and we swam like that together. She was still laughing. On the quayside, while we were drying off, she said: 'I'm more tanned than you.' I asked her if she wanted to go to the movies that night. She laughed again and said she wanted to see a film with Fernandel in it. After we were dressed, she seemed very surprised to see me wearing a black tie and asked if I was in mourning. I told her that Mama had died. She wanted to know when it had happened, so I said: 'Yesterday.' She flinched a little but didn't say anything. I wanted to tell her that it wasn't my fault, but I stopped myself because I remembered I'd already said that to my boss. That doesn't mean anything. Although actually, everyone is always a little guilty.

By the evening, Marie had forgotten all about it. The movie was funny in parts but then got really ridiculous. She pressed her leg against mine. I stroked her breasts. Towards the end of the movie, I kissed her, but awkwardly. After we left, she came back to my place.

When I woke up, Marie had gone. She'd told me she had to visit her aunt. I realized it was Sunday, which annoyed me; I don't like Sundays. I turned over in my bed to see if I could still smell the salt from Marie's hair in the pillow and went back to sleep until ten o'clock. Then I smoked in bed until noon. I didn't want to have lunch at Céleste's as I usually did because he was bound to ask me all sorts of questions and I don't like it when people do that. I cooked myself some eggs and ate them straight out of the frying pan with no bread because there wasn't any left and I didn't feel like going out to buy some.

After lunch, I was a bit bored and I wandered around the large apartment. It was practical when Mama was here. Now the place is too big for me, so I've moved the dining table into my bedroom. I only live in this one room now with a few slightly sagging wicker chairs, the closet with its yellowing mirror, a dressing table and the brass bed. Everything else has been left where it was. A little while later, because I had nothing else to do, I picked up an old newspaper and read it. I cut out an ad for Kruschen Salts and glued it into an old notebook where I keep things from the papers I find amusing. Then I washed my hands and finally went out on to the balcony.

My bedroom looks out over the main street of the neighbourhood. It was a beautiful afternoon. But the pavements were slippery and the few people who passed by were in a hurry. They were mainly families who'd gone out for a walk: two little boys wearing sailor suits with shorts that stopped above the knee – they looked a little awkward in their formal clothes – and a little girl with a large pink bow in her hair and black patent-leather shoes. Behind them was their mother, an enormous woman in a brown silk dress, and their father, a rather frail-looking, short man I'd seen before. He wore a boater and a bow tie and carried a walking stick. Seeing him with his wife, I understood why people in the neighbourhood said he looked distinguished.

A little while later, some local young men passed by: slicked-back hair, red ties, very tight jackets with embroidered handkerchiefs sticking out of their pockets and shoes with square toes. I thought they were probably going to see a movie in town. That was why they were leaving so early and laughing so much as they hurried to catch the tram.

After they'd gone, the street gradually became deserted. The shows had all started, I suppose. Only the shopkeepers and a few cats were left in the street. The sky was clear but not very bright above the ficus trees that lined the road. On the pavement opposite, the tobacconist brought out a chair, put it in front of his door and straddled it, resting both arms on its back. The trams that had been jam-packed just a short while ago were now almost empty. In the little café called 'Chez Pierrot', next to the tobacco shop, the waiter was sweeping up sawdust in the empty room. It was truly a Sunday.

I turned my chair around the way the tobacconist did because I found it more comfortable like that. I smoked two more cigarettes, went inside for a piece of chocolate and came back and stood next to the window to eat it. A little while later, the sky grew darker and I thought we might have one of those summer storms. It gradually cleared up again though. But the passing clouds had left the threat of rain hovering above the street, making it look more dismal. I stood and watched the sky for a long time.

The trams came back at five o'clock, making a lot of noise. They had been to the sports stadium in the suburbs and carried groups of spectators who were huddled on the running boards and hanging on to the guardrails. The next trams were full of the players; I recognized them by their sports bags. They were shouting and singing at the top of their lungs – their club would go on forever. Several of them waved to me. One of them even shouted out: 'We thrashed them!' And I nodded my head as if to say 'Yes'. After that, more and more traffic began streaming by.

Some time passed. Above the rooftops, the sky grew reddish and as night fell the streets started filling up. The people who'd gone for a walk came back, a few at a time. I recognized the distinguished-looking man amongst the others. The children were either crying or letting themselves be dragged along. The local cinemas suddenly let a wave of spectators out into the street, all at the same time. Some of the young men were more animated than usual, which made me think they'd seen a thriller. The people coming back from the movies in town arrived a bit later. They looked more serious. They were laughing, but only every now and again; they seemed tired and preoccupied. They lingered in the street, coming and going on the pavement opposite. The young girls from the neighbourhood walked arm in arm; they weren't wearing hats. The young men positioned themselves so the girls would have to pass directly by them; they made friendly remarks to the girls but they just laughed and looked away. Several of the ones I knew waved at me.

Then the street lamps suddenly came on, softening the first stars that appeared in the night sky. I felt my eyes starting to hurt after watching the streets with their lights and masses of people for so long. The street lamps made the damp pavements glisten and every few minutes the headlights of the trams lit up someone's shiny hair, a smile or a silver bracelet. A little while later, as the trams passed by less and less often, the night grew even darker above the trees and lights, and the streets below began to empty little by little, until the first cat slowly crossed the road, deserted once more. Then I thought I should have some supper. My neck hurt a little from leaning over the back of the chair for such a long time. I went out to buy some bread and pasta, prepared my meal and ate it standing up. I wanted to smoke another cigarette at the window but it was chilly now and I felt a little cold. I closed the windows. As I stepped back into the room, I saw, reflected in the mirror, the edge of the table where some bits of bread lay next to my oil lamp. I thought that it was one more Sunday nearly over and done with, that Mama was now dead and buried, that I would go back to work, and that when all was said and done, nothing had really changed.

# 3

I worked hard at the office today. My boss was nice to me. He asked me if I wasn't too tired and also wanted to know how old Mama was. I said 'in her sixties' so I wouldn't make a mistake, and I don't know why, but he seemed relieved and to consider the matter closed.

Bills of lading were piled up in a stack on my desk and I had to go through them all. At twelve o'clock, I washed my hands before leaving the office for lunch. I like this moment of the day. In the evening, it's not as nice because the roller towel is soaking wet: it's been used all day long. I once pointed this out to my boss. He replied that he was sorry but that in the end it was a minor detail and not important. I went out a little late, at twelve-thirty, with Emmanuel, who works in the shipping department. The office looks out over the sea and we spent a moment watching the cargo ships in the port bathed in the scorching hot sun. Just then, a truck arrived with a racket of rattling chains and what sounded like explosions from its engine. Emmanuel asked me if 'we should go for it' and I started to run. The truck rushed past and we chased after it. I was blinded by the noise and the dust. I could barely see a thing and all I felt was the exhilarating rush as I sped between the winches and machinery, past the masts of the ships bobbing up and down in the distance and the hulls of the boats. I took a huge leap and managed to jump on to the truck first. Then I helped Emmanuel climb up. We were gasping for breath as the truck bumped along the uneven cobblestones of the quayside, amid the sun and the dust. Emmanuel was laughing so hard he could hardly breathe.

By the time we got to Céleste's, we were dripping with sweat. He was always there, with his fat stomach, his apron and his white moustache. He asked me if 'I was all right what with everything'. I said yes and told him I was hungry. I ate very quickly and then had a coffee. Then I went home and slept a little because I'd had too much wine with lunch, and when I woke up, I felt like having a cigarette. It was late and I ran to catch the tram. I worked all afternoon. It was very hot in the office and in the evening, when I left, I was glad to walk slowly back home along the quayside. The sky was a delicate green; I felt happy. I went straight home, though, because I wanted to make myself some boiled potatoes.

As I was walking up the stairs, I ran into old Salamano, a neighbour who lives on the same floor as me. He was with his dog. He's had him for eight years and they're always together. The spaniel has a skin disease – mange, I think it's called – which makes him lose almost all his hair and leaves him covered in reddish patches and brown scabs. Because they've lived alone together for so long in one little room, old Salamano has ended up looking like his dog. He also has reddish scabs on his face and yellowish, thinning hair. As for the dog, he's taken on some of his owner's characteristics: hunched up, with his muzzle sticking out and his neck tensed. They look like they're related and yet they hate each other. Twice a day, at eleven o'clock and six o'clock, the old man takes his dog out for a walk; for eight years, they haven't changed their routine. You can see them walking down the Rue de Lyon, the dog pulling Salamano until the old man trips. So he hits the dog and curses him. The frightened dog slows down and lets himself be dragged along. Then the old man has to tug him. As soon as the dog has forgotten, he pulls his master again and he's again cursed and beaten. Then the two of them stand still on the pavement and look at each other, the dog with terror, the man with hatred. It's the same every day. When the dog wants to urinate, the old man doesn't give him enough time to finish and pulls at his leash so the dog leaves a trail of little drops behind him. If the dog accidentally pees in the room, he's beaten again. It's been going on like this for eight years. Céleste always says: 'It's awful', but when all is said and done, no one really knows. When I ran into him on the stairs, Salamano was cursing his dog. He called him 'Bastard!' and 'Dirty swine!' and the dog was whimpering. I said: 'Good evening', but the old man kept on shouting at the dog. So I asked him what the dog had done to him. He didn't reply. All he said was 'Bastard!' and 'Dirty swine!' I could see he was bent over the dog, trying to untangle something from his collar. I spoke louder. Then, without turning round, he replied with a sort of repressed rage: 'He's always there.' Then he left, pulling the dog behind him, and the dog let himself be dragged along, whimpering.

Just then my other neighbour came in. Rumour has it around here that he lives off women. But when you ask him what he does, he says he works in a 'warehouse'. On the whole, he's not very well liked. But he often talks to me and sometimes he drops by for a while because I listen to him. I find what he says interesting. And besides, I don't have any reason not to talk to him. His name is Raymond Sintès. He's rather short, with broad shoulders and a boxer's nose. He's always very well dressed. Once, when we were talking about Salamano, he also said: 'It's awful!' He asked me if I thought it was disgusting and I said no.

We walked upstairs and I was about to say goodbye to him when he said: 'I've got some black pudding and wine. Would you like to have a bite to eat with me?' I thought how I wouldn't have to cook dinner and said yes. He also has only one room and a kitchen with no window. On the wall above his bed there's a pink-and-white stucco angel, some pictures of sporting champions and two or three snap-shots of naked women. The room was dirty and he hadn't made the bed. First he lit the oil lamp, then he took a rather grimy-looking bandage out of his pocket and wrapped up his right hand with it. I asked him what had happened. He told me he'd been in a fight with some guy who'd been ask-ing for trouble.

'You have to understand, Monsieur Meursault,' he said, 'I'm not a bad sort but I do have a quick temper. So this guy says to me: "If you're really a man, you'll get off this tram." So I say: "Come on now, don't get so worked up." Then he calls me a coward. So I get off the tram and tell him: "That's enough now. Cut it out or I'll let you have it." Then he says: "You and who else?" So I punched him. He fell down. I was about to help him up but he started kicking me while he was still on the ground. So I hit him with my knee and punched him a few times. His face was all bloody. Then I asked him if he'd had enough. He said: "Yes."' The whole time he was talking, Sintès was bandaging his hand. I was sitting on the bed. 'You can see that I wasn't looking for trouble,' he said. 'He's the one who started it.' That was true and I said so. Then he told me that actually he wanted my advice about the whole business, that I was a man, I understood life, I could help him and afterwards he'd be my friend. I didn't reply. He asked me again if I'd like to be his friend. I told him I didn't mind; he seemed pleased. He took out the black pudding and started cooking it in a frying pan; he put out the glasses, plates, cutlery and two bottles of wine. All in silence. Then we sat down at the table. While we were eating, he started telling me his story. At first he hesitated a little. 'I used to know this woman ... I guess you could say she was my mistress ...' The man he'd had the fight with was the woman's brother. He told me that he'd been keeping her. I didn't say anything and right away he added that he knew what people said about him in the neighbourhood but he worked in a warehouse and had a clear conscience.

'But to get on with my story,' he said, 'I realized she was cheating on me.' He gave her just enough money to live on. He even paid her rent and gave her twenty francs a day for food. 'Three hundred francs for her room, six hundred for food, a pair of stockings now and again – that came to about a thousand francs. And, needless to say, Madame didn't work. But she told me she couldn't get by on what I gave her. So I asked her: "Why not get a job, just part time? That would help me out because all those other little things add up. I bought you a new outfit this month, I give you twenty francs a day, I pay your rent and what do you do? You have coffee in the afternoon with your friends. You offer them

27

coffee and sugar while I'm the one giving you money. I've been good to you but you haven't been good to me." But she didn't go out to work, she kept saying that she couldn't and that's when I realized she must be cheating on me.'

Then he told me how he'd found a lottery ticket in her bag and how she couldn't explain where she'd got the money to buy it. A little later he'd found a pawn ticket she'd been given as a receipt for two bracelets. Up until then, he didn't even know she owned any bracelets. 'That's when I knew for sure she'd been cheating on me. So I left her. But first, I hit her. Then I told her the truth about herself. I told her that all she really wanted was to get laid and it didn't matter by whom. You understand, Monsieur Meursault, I told her: "You don't see how jealous everyone is of how happy I've made you. You'll realize later on how happy you were with me."'

He'd beaten her up badly. Before then, he'd never hit her. 'I'd slapped her a little, but affectionately, so to speak. She'd cry out a little. Then I'd close the shutters and it would finish the way it always did. But now it's serious. And as far as I'm concerned, I haven't punished her enough.'

Then he explained that it was why he needed my advice. He stopped talking to fix the wick on the oil lamp, which was turning black. I just sat and listened to him. I'd drunk nearly a whole bottle of wine and my forehead felt very hot. I smoked some of Raymond's cigarettes because I didn't have any left. The last trams passed by, carrying away the distant sounds of the suburbs. Raymond continued talking. What bothered him was that he still had sexual feelings for her. But he wanted to punish her. First he'd thought he'd take her to a hotel and call the Vice Squad to cause a scandal and have her officially registered as a prostitute. Then he'd gone to see some shady friends of his. They couldn't come up with anything. And as Raymond pointed out to me, petty criminals were never much use. He'd told them the same thing and then they'd suggested 'branding' her. But he didn't like that idea. He needed to think about it. First, however, he wanted to ask me something. Before he did, though, he wanted to know what I thought about the whole business. I told him I didn't have any opinion about it, but that I found it interesting.

First he asked me if I thought she'd been cheating on him and I said that yes, it seemed so to me, then if I thought she should be punished and what I would do if I were him, so I told him that you can never know for sure, but I could understand that he wanted to punish her. I drank a bit more wine. He lit a cigarette and told me his plan. He wanted to write her a letter, one that would 'hit her hard but at the same time say things that would make her sorry and miss him'. Then, after she came back to him, he'd sleep with her and as soon as he'd finished, he'd spit in her face and throw her out. I told him I thought that would really be a way to punish her. But Raymond said he didn't think he would be able to write the kind of letter he needed, so he'd thought of asking me to do it. When I didn't reply, he asked me if I would mind doing it right then and there. And I agreed.

He drank another glass of wine and stood up. He pushed aside our plates and the bit of black pudding we hadn't finished. He carefully cleaned the plastic tablecloth. He got a sheet of lined paper out of the drawer of his bedside table, along with a yellow envelope, a little penholder made of red wood and a square inkwell filled with purple ink. When he told me the woman's name, I realized she was an Arab. I wrote the letter. I more or less improvised, but I tried to write it in a way that would make Raymond happy because I had no reason not to make him happy. Then I read out the letter. He smoked a cigarette as he listened, nodding his head, then asked me to read it out again. He was really pleased with it. 'I could tell you understood life,' he said warmly. At first I didn't realize he'd started addressing me in a very personal way. It only struck me when he said: 'Now, we're really pals.' He said the same thing again and I said: 'Yes.' It didn't matter to me one way or the other whether we were friends or not, but it really seemed to matter to him. He put the letter in the envelope and we finished the wine. Then we sat there for a while, smoking in silence. Outside, everything was quiet and we could hear the sound of a car passing by. I said: 'It's late.' Raymond thought so too. He remarked that time passed quickly and, in a certain way, that was true. I was tired and found it difficult to get up. I must have looked tired because Raymond said I should take better care of myself. At first I didn't understand. Then he said he'd heard that Mama had died but it was something that was bound to happen one day. That was how I felt too.

I stood up, Raymond shook my hand very hard and said that we men always understood each other. I closed his door behind me when I left and stood on the landing for a moment in the dark. Everything was quiet and I could feel a damp breeze rising up from the stairwell below. All I could hear was the blood pulsating and humming in my ears. I stood very still. But in Salamano's room, the dog was whimpering softly.

# 4

I worked hard all week. Raymond came to see me and said he'd sent the letter. I went to the movies twice with Emmanuel, who doesn't always understand what he sees on the screen, so I have to explain everything to him. Yesterday was Saturday and Marie came over as we'd arranged. I really wanted to sleep with her because she was wearing a pretty dress with red and white stripes and leather sandals. You could see the outline of her firm breasts and her sun-tanned face made her look radiant. We took a bus and travelled a few kilometres outside of Algiers to a beach that was nestled between some rocks, with reeds along the inland side. The late afternoon sun wasn't very hot, but the water was warm, with lazy, long, low waves. Marie taught me a game. While we were swimming, we had to drink in the tops of the waves and gather all the foam we could into our mouths; then we had to turn over and float on our backs while spraying the water up towards the sky. The foam was frothy and disappeared into the air or fell back on to my face like warm rain. But after a while my mouth burned from the bitter salt. Marie came over to me and pressed her body against mine in the water. She kissed me. Her tongue felt cool against my lips and we floated along, carried by the waves for a while.

After we got dressed on the beach, Marie looked at me; her eyes were shining. I kissed her. We didn't say anything more. I held her close and all we wanted to do was catch a bus, go home and throw ourselves down on my bed. I'd left my window open and it felt good to feel the summer night flowing over our tanned bodies.

That morning, Marie stayed and I told her we could have lunch together. I went downstairs to buy some meat. On my way back upstairs, I heard a woman's voice in Raymond's room. A little later, Salamano was shouting at his dog; we heard the sound of footsteps and the dog's paws scratching the wooden stairs and then 'Bastard, dirty swine' as they went out into the street. I told Marie all about the old man and she laughed. She was wearing one of my pyjama tops with the sleeves rolled up. When she laughed, I wanted her again. A moment later, she asked me if I loved her. I told her that didn't mean anything, but I didn't think so. She looked sad then. But while we were making lunch, she laughed again, for no apparent reason, and the way she laughed made me kiss her. At that very moment, we heard a fight break out in Raymond's place.

First we heard the high-pitched voice of a woman and then Raymond saying: 'You cheated on me, you humiliated me. I'll teach you to cheat on me.' Then we heard a few muffled sounds, followed by the woman screaming so horribly that in a flash everyone rushed out on to the landing. Marie and I also went out. The woman kept screaming and Raymond kept on hitting her. Marie said it was awful and I didn't reply. She asked me to go and get a policeman and I told her I didn't like the police. But then one of them showed up with the plumber who lives on the second

floor. He knocked on the door and everything went quiet.
He banged on it harder and, after a moment, the woman
started crying and Raymond opened the door. He was
smoking a cigarette and looked smug. The young woman
rushed to the door and told the policeman that Raymond
had beaten her. 'Name,' said the policeman. Raymond told
him. 'Take that cigarette out of your mouth when you're
talking to me.' Raymond hesitated, glanced over at me and
took another drag of his cigarette. When he did that, the
policeman slapped him so hard across the face that you
could hear it; his cigarette went flying. Raymond turned
pale but didn't say anything for a moment and then meekly
asked if he could pick up his cigarette butt. The policeman
said he could, then added: 'But next time, you'll remember
that the police aren't idiots.' While this was going on, the
young woman was crying and saying: 'He hit me. He's a
pimp' over and over again. Then Raymond said: 'Tell me,
officer, isn't it against the law to call a man a pimp?' But the
policeman replied: 'Shut your trap.' Then Raymond turned
to the girl and said: 'Just you wait, you haven't seen the last
of me.' The policeman told him to shut up and said that the
girl should leave and that he should stay put until he was
told to come down to the police station. He added that Raymond should be ashamed of being so drunk that he was
shaking. Then Raymond said: 'I'm not drunk, officer. It's
just that here I am, standing in front of you, and of course
I'm shaking, I can't help it.' He closed the door and everyone left. Marie and I finished making lunch. But she wasn't
hungry; I ate nearly all of it. She left at one o'clock and I
slept for a while.

Around three o'clock, Raymond knocked on my door

and came inside. I was still lying down. He sat on the edge of the bed. He didn't say anything at first and I asked him how it had gone. He told me he had done what he'd planned but that then she'd slapped him across the face so he'd started hitting her. I'd seen what happened next. I told him that it seemed to me that she'd been punished and that he should be satisfied. That was also his opinion and he pointed out that it didn't matter what the policeman had done because it wouldn't change the fact that he'd given her a beating. Then he added that he knew what cops were like and just how to deal with them. Then he asked me if I'd expected him to hit the policeman back after he'd been slapped. I replied that I hadn't expected anything at all and that, besides, I didn't like the police. Raymond seemed very pleased. He asked me if I wanted to go out somewhere with him. I got up and combed my hair. He told me that I had to be a witness for him. As far as I was concerned, it didn't matter in the least but I didn't know what he wanted me to say. According to Raymond, all I had to do was say that the girl had cheated on him. So I agreed to be a witness for him.

We went out and Raymond bought me a brandy. Then he wanted to play billiards and I nearly won. Afterwards, he wanted to go to a brothel but I said no because I don't like that kind of thing. So we walked slowly back home and he told me how happy he was that he'd managed to punish his mistress. He was being very kind to me and I thought it was a nice moment.

In the distance, I noticed old Salamano standing at the doorway, looking upset. When we got closer, I saw that his dog wasn't with him. He was looking everywhere, turning round in circles, trying to see inside the dark hallway, mumbling incoherently, then peering down the street with his little red eyes. When Raymond asked him what was wrong, he didn't answer right away. I could just about make out what he was saying – 'Bastard, dirty swine' – and that he was getting all worked up. I asked him where his dog was. He answered me sharply, saying he'd run away. And then, suddenly, he started talking very quickly: 'I took him to the Parade Ground, as usual. It was very crowded because of the fair stalls. I stopped to have a look at the "King of the Escape Artists". And when I was ready to leave, he was gone. Of course, I'd been meaning to buy him a smaller collar for a long time. But I never would have believed that dirty swine would run away like that.'

Then Raymond said that the dog must have got lost and that he'd come back. He gave him lots of examples of dogs that had travelled dozens of miles to make their way back home. In spite of that, the old man seemed even more upset. 'But they'll take him away from me, don't you understand? It wouldn't be so bad if I thought someone might take him in. But that's impossible; he disgusts everyone with his scabs. The police will pick him up, for sure.' So I told him that all he had to do was go down to the pound and he'd get him back after he'd paid a fee. He asked me if the fee was very expensive. I didn't know. Then he got angry: 'Pay good money for that little bastard. Ah! He can go to hell!' And he started cursing him. Raymond laughed and went inside the house. I followed him in and we said goodbye on the landing. A moment later, I heard the old man's footsteps and he knocked on my door. When I opened it, he just stood there for a moment then finally said: 'I'm sorry. I'm sorry.' I asked him if he wanted to come in, but he said no. He was staring at his feet and his scabby hands were shaking. Without looking at me, he asked: 'Tell me, Monsieur Meursault, they won't take him away from me. They'll give him back to me. Otherwise, what will happen to me?' I told him that the pound kept dogs for three days in case their owners came for them and that afterwards they did what they thought best. He looked at me in silence. Then he said: 'Good night.' He closed his door and I could hear him walking back and forth. His bed creaked. And when I heard a strange little sound coming from the other side of the wall, I realized he was crying. I don't know why, but I thought of Mama. But I had to get up early the next day. I wasn't hungry and I went to bed without dinner.

# 5

Raymond called me at the office. He said that one of his friends (he'd told him about me) had invited me to spend Sunday at his beach house, near Algiers. I said I'd like that very much but that I'd promised to spend the day with my girlfriend. Raymond immediately said she was also invited. His friend's wife would be very happy not to be the only woman in a group of men.

I wanted to hang up right away because I know that my boss doesn't like us getting personal phone calls. But Raymond asked me to wait a moment and he said he could have told me about the invitation that evening but he wanted to warn me about something else. His former mistress's brother and a group of his Arab friends had been following him all day. 'If you see him near the house tonight when you get home, let me know.' I said I would.

A little while later, my boss asked to see me and I was annoyed at first because I thought he was going to tell me I should spend less time talking on the phone and more time working. But it wasn't about that at all. He said he wanted to speak to me about a project that was still in the planning stages. He'd just like my opinion on the matter. He was thinking of setting up an office in Paris where they could deal directly with the large companies they did business with there; he wanted to know if I'd be interested in going there to work. It would mean I could live in Paris and also travel part of the year. 'You're young and it seems to me it might be the kind of life you'd enjoy.' I said yes, but that, actually, I didn't care one way or the other. Then he asked me whether I would be interested in changing my life. I replied that you can never really change your life and that, in any case, every life was more or less the same and that my life here wasn't bad at all. He looked displeased, told me I could never give a straight answer, that I had no ambition and that this was disastrous in business. So I went back to work. I would have preferred not to upset him, but I could see no reason to change my life. After giving it serious thought, I wasn't unhappy. When I was a student, I was very ambitious about having a career. But when I had to give up my studies, I realized quite soon that none of that sort of thing mattered very much.

That evening, Marie came to see me and asked me if I wanted to marry her. I said that it was all the same to me and that we could get married if she wanted to. Then she wanted to know if I loved her. I replied as I had once before that that didn't mean anything, but said I was pretty sure I didn't love her. 'Why marry me, then?' she asked. I explained that it was of no importance whatsoever but if that was what she wanted, we could get married. And besides, she was the one asking and I was happy to say yes. She then remarked that marriage was a serious business. I said: 'Not at all.' She said nothing for a moment, just looked at me in silence. Then she spoke. She simply wanted to know if I would say yes to any other woman who asked me, if I were involved with her in the same way. I said: 'Of course.' She then wondered if she loved me, but there was no way I could know anything about that. After another moment's silence, she murmured that I was very strange, that she undoubtedly loved me for that very reason, but that one day she might find me repulsive, for the same reason. When I said nothing, because I had nothing more to say, she smiled, put her arm through mine and said that she wanted to marry me. I said we could do it as soon as she wanted. Then I told her about my boss's plan and Marie said she'd like to get to know Paris. I told her that I'd lived there for a while and she asked me what it was like. 'It's dirty,' I replied. 'There are pigeons and dark courtyards. Everyone looks pale.'

Then we went for a walk in the city along the wide avenues. The women we saw were all beautiful and I asked Marie if she'd noticed that. She said she had and that she understood me. For a while, we didn't speak. I wanted her to stay with me, though, and I told her we could eat together at Céleste's. She really wanted to, but she had things to do. We were nearly back at my place and I said goodbye to her. She looked at me: 'Don't you want to know what I have to do?' I did want to know, but I hadn't thought to ask, which was why she seemed to be reproaching me. Then, when she saw I was getting tied up in knots trying to explain, she laughed again and leaned her body in towards mine so I could kiss her.

I had dinner at Céleste's. I'd already started eating when a very strange little woman came in and asked if she could share my table. Of course she could. She had sharp, jerky gestures and bright eyes in a small round face. She took off her jacket, sat down and started busily studying the menu. She called Céleste over and immediately ordered everything she wanted in a hurried but precise tone of voice. While waiting for her first course, she opened her bag and took out a little notebook and a pencil, added up what her bill would come to, then took out her purse and placed enough money to cover the exact amount of the bill, including the tip, on the table in front of her. Just then, her first course arrived, which she wolfed down very quickly. While waiting for the next course, she took a blue pencil out of her bag and a magazine that listed the week's radio shows. Very carefully, she placed a tick beside almost every programme, one by one. Since the magazine was about twelve pages long, she continued her meticulous work throughout the entire meal. I had already finished eating and she was still totally engrossed in making her notes. Then she stood up, put her jacket back on with the same precise, robotic movements and left. Since I had nothing to do, I also left and followed her for a little while. She'd walked to the edge of the pavement and with unbelievable speed and concentration she headed down the road in a straight line without looking back. Eventually, I lost sight of her and I turned around and walked home. I thought that she was very strange but soon forgot about her.

I found old Salamano standing in front of my door. I showed him in and he told me that his dog was really gone; he wasn't at the pound. The employees there had told him that the dog had perhaps been run over. He'd asked if he could find out for sure at the police station. He was told that they didn't keep records of such things because they happened every day. I told Salamano that he could get another dog, but he was right in pointing out that he was used to his.

I was sitting on the edge of my bed and Salamano was on

a chair by the table. He was facing me and had his hands on his knees. He'd kept his old felt hat on. It was hard to understand him because he was mumbling beneath his yellowish moustache. He bored me a little but I had nothing to do and I wasn't tired yet. Just to say something, I asked him about his dog. He told me he'd got him after his wife died. He got married rather late in life. When he was young, he wanted to work in the theatre: when he was in the army, he acted in vaudeville to entertain the troops. But he ended up working on the railways and he had no regrets because he now had a small pension. He hadn't been happy with his wife but in the end he'd got used to being with her. When she died, he'd felt very lonely. So he asked one of his workmates for a dog and had got him when he was still a puppy. He had to feed it with a baby's bottle. But since dogs don't live as long as people, they'd ended up growing old together. 'He was bad-tempered,' old Salamano told me. 'From time to time, we'd have it out. But he was a good dog all the same.' I said he was a good breed and Salamano seemed pleased. 'And you didn't even know him before he got sick,' he added. 'His coat used to be the most beautiful thing about him.' Every morning and every evening after the dog got the skin disease, Salamano rubbed ointment on him. But according to Salamano, his real disease was old age, and you can't cure old age.

I yawned just then and the old man said he'd go. I told him he could stay and that I was sorry about what had happened to his dog; he thanked me. He told me that Mama had liked his dog a lot. When he mentioned her, he called her 'your poor mother'. He hinted that I must be very unhappy since Mama died, but I didn't reply. He then said very quickly and sounding rather embarrassed that he knew that people in the neighbourhood thought badly of me because I'd put my mother in a home, but he knew me and he knew that I'd loved Mama a lot. I replied – I still don't know why – that I hadn't been aware people had criticized me about that, but sending Mama to the home had seemed the natural thing to do since I didn't earn enough to pay someone to take care of her. 'And besides,' I added, 'for a long time she didn't have anything to talk to me about and she was bored all by herself.' 'Yes,' he said, 'and at least at the home you make friends.' Then he said he'd be going. He wanted to get to bed. His life had changed now and he didn't quite know what he was going to do. For the first time since I'd known him, he shyly offered me his hand, and when I shook it, I could feel the scales on his skin. He gave me a little smile; as he was leaving, he said: 'I hope the dogs won't bark tonight. I always think that one of them is mine.'

# 6

On Sunday, I found it difficult to wake up and Marie had to call my name and shake me. We didn't eat because we wanted to go for an early swim. I felt completely empty and my head hurt a little. My cigarette tasted bitter. Marie made fun of me because she said I 'looked like death'. She had put on a white linen dress and left her hair down. I told her she was beautiful; she laughed and sounded pleased.

On the way downstairs we knocked on Raymond's door. He called out that he was coming. Out in the street the sun was already so hot that, because I was tired and also because we'd kept the shutters closed, it felt like a slap across the face. Marie was really excited and kept on saying what a beautiful day it was. I was feeling a bit better and realized I was hungry. I said so to Marie and she pointed to the beach bag where she'd put our bathing suits and towel. I would have to wait; then we heard Raymond closing his door. He was wearing blue trousers and a short-sleeved white shirt. But he'd put on a boater, which made Marie laugh, and his skin was very white under the dark hair on his forearms. I found it a little repulsive. He was whistling as he came down the stairs and looked very happy. He said: 'Hello, old boy' to me and called Marie 'Mademoiselle'.

The day before, we'd gone to the police station and I'd

43

given my statement, saying that the woman had been 'disrespectful' towards Raymond. He got off with a warning. No one had verified my statement. While we were standing by the door, we talked about it for a bit with Raymond, then we decided to take the bus. The beach wasn't far but we'd get there faster that way. Raymond thought his friend would be pleased if we got there early. We were just about to leave when Raymond suddenly gestured to me to look across the street. I saw a group of Arabs leaning against the window of the tobacco shop. They were watching us in silence, but in a way that was particular to them, looking through us as if we were rocks or dead trees. Raymond said that the guy second from the left was the one he'd told me about; he seemed worried. But then he added that it was all ancient history now. Marie didn't understand what was going on and asked us what was wrong. I told her they were Arabs who had a grudge against Raymond. She wanted us to leave right away. Raymond stood up tall and laughed, saying we'd better hurry up.

We headed for the bus stop a bit further along and Raymond said that the Arabs weren't following us. I turned around. They hadn't moved; they just kept staring at the same spot with the same air of indifference. We got on the bus. Raymond, who seemed enormously relieved, told Marie one joke after the other. I got the feeling he was attracted to her, but she barely said a word to him. Every now and again, she would look at him and laugh.

We got off in the suburbs of Algiers. The beach wasn't far from the bus stop. But we had to walk across a little ridge that looked out over the sea and then dropped steeply down to the beach. It was covered in yellowish rocks and dazzling white asphodels that stood out sharply against the relentless blue of the sky. Marie thought it was fun to scatter their petals by swinging at them with her beach bag. We walked through rows of little houses with green or white fences; some of them had verandas and were hidden by tamarisk bushes, others stood starkly amid the rocks. Before reaching the edge of the ridge, we could already make out the still sea and, further away, an enormous deserted promontory in the clear water. We could hear the distant sound of a motor through the quiet air. Then we saw a little trawler in the distance, inching its way towards us over the bright, luminous sea. Marie picked some small irises that grew between the rocks. From the steep slope leading down towards the sea, we could see that a few people were already in the water.

Raymond's friend lived in a little wooden chalet at the other end of the beach. The house was built against the rocks but its supports at the front were already below water level. Raymond introduced us. His friend was called Masson. He was a tall man, enormous, with very broad shoulders; his wife was plump and friendly with a Parisian accent. He told us to make ourselves at home and that they were frying up some fish he'd caught that very morning. I told him how pretty I thought his house was. He said that he spent Saturdays and Sundays and every day off there. 'My wife gets on very well with people,' he added. Just then, Marie and his wife started laughing together. It was perhaps the first time I realized I was actually going to get married.

Masson wanted to go swimming but his wife and Raymond didn't want to come along. The three of us went down to the beach and Marie jumped straight into the

45

water. Masson and I waited a bit. Masson spoke slowly and I noticed he had the habit of ending everything he said with 'and what's more', even when he was actually adding nothing that changed the meaning of what he'd already said. About Marie, he remarked: 'She's terrific, and what's more, charming.' Then I stopped paying attention to this little mannerism because I was thinking about how wonderful it was to be out in the sun and how good it felt. The sand was starting to feel warm under my feet. Despite my eagerness to get into the water, I resisted for a while longer but finally said to Masson: 'Ready?' I dived in. Masson walked slowly into the water and only started swimming when it was too deep to keep walking. He was doing the breaststroke, and rather badly, so I left him on his own and went to join Marie. The water was cold and I was happy to be swimming. Marie and I swam far out, moving in harmony with each other and happy to be together.

Once we were out in the open, we floated on our backs, and as I gazed up at the sky, the sun dried away the last of the water that trickled down my face into my mouth. We saw that Masson had gone back on to the beach to stretch out in the sun. Even from a distance, he looked enormous. Marie wanted us to swim together. I got behind her so I could hold her around the waist and she swam forward using her arms while I helped her by kicking my legs. The gentle sound of the splashing water in the morning light stayed with us for some time, until I got tired. Then I left Marie where she was and swam back at a normal pace, taking deep breaths. I stretched out on my stomach on the beach near Masson and rested my head on the sand. I told him 'It felt good' and he agreed. A little while later, Marie came out of the water. I turned around to watch her walk towards us. She was covered in a film of salty water and was holding her hair back. She lay down, pressing her thigh against mine, and the heat from our two bodies and the sun made me feel drowsy.

Marie gave me a shake and told me that Masson had gone back to the house because it was time for lunch. I got up right away because I was hungry and Marie said I hadn't kissed her since that morning. That was true, but I hadn't felt like it. 'Come into the water,' she said. We ran and splashed through the shallow little waves. We swam for a while and then she pressed her body against mine. I felt her legs wrapped around mine and I wanted her.

When we came out of the water, Masson was already calling us. I said I was very hungry and right away he told his wife that he liked me. The bread was good; I wolfed down my fish. Then we had some meat and fried potatoes. We all ate in silence. Masson drank a lot of wine and kept filling my glass. By the time we were having coffee, my head felt heavy and I'd smoked a lot of cigarettes. Masson, Raymond and I talked about how we might spend the month of August together at the beach, sharing the expenses. Suddenly, Marie said: 'Do you know what time it is? It's only eleven-thirty.' We were all surprised, but Masson said that we'd eaten very early but that was natural because the time to eat is when you're hungry. I don't know why that made Marie laugh. I think she may have had a bit too much to drink. Then Masson asked me if I wanted to go for a walk on the beach with him. 'My wife always takes a nap after lunch. But I don't like to. I need a walk. I keep telling her it's healthier. But in the end, it's up to her.' Marie said she'd stay to help Masson's wife with the dishes. The little Parisian woman said we men had to leave so they could clear up. The three of us went out.

The sun was beating down on the sand and its brilliance reflecting off the sea was almost unbearable. The beach was deserted now. We could hear the clinking sound of cutlery and dishes from the beach houses along the ridge that led down to the sea. The heat rising from the rocks and the ground made it difficult to breathe. At first Raymond and Masson talked about things and people I didn't know. I realized they'd known each other for a long time and had even shared a place for a while. We headed towards the sea and walked along the water's edge. Every now and then a little wave that was longer than the last one wet our canvas shoes. My mind was a blank because all that sun on my bare head was making me feel drowsy.

Just then, Raymond said something to Masson that I couldn't make out. But at the same time, I noticed two Arabs wearing blue workman's overalls coming towards us; they were at the other end of the beach, still quite far away. I looked at Raymond and he said: 'It's him.' We carried on walking. Masson asked how they'd managed to follow us all the way here. I realized they must have seen us get on the bus with a beach bag, but I didn't say anything.

Even though the Arabs were moving slowly, they were now a lot closer to us. We kept walking at the same pace but Raymond said: 'If there's a fight, you take the second one, Masson. I'll take care of mine. If another one shows up, Meursault, he's yours.' I said 'Yes', and Masson put his hands in his pockets. The sand was now so scorching hot it looked red. We walked steadily forward towards the Arabs.

We were getting closer and closer. When they were a few steps away from us, the Arabs stopped. Masson and I had slowed down. Raymond walked straight up to his man. I couldn't make out what Raymond said to him, but the Arab made a menacing gesture as if he was going to punch him in the face. So Raymond hit him first and immediately called out for Masson. Masson went over to the second one and hit him twice with all his strength. The Arab fell face down into the water and stayed there for a few seconds, little bubbles rising to the surface around his head. Meanwhile, Raymond had hit the other Arab, whose face was covered in blood. Raymond turned around to me and said: 'Just you watch what I'm going to do to him.' I shouted: 'Look out, he's got a knife!' But by then, Raymond's arm was already cut and his mouth slashed.

Masson leaped forward but the other Arab got up and was standing behind the one with the knife. We didn't dare move. They walked slowly backwards, staring at us, keeping us at a distance by wielding the knife. When they saw there was enough distance between us, they ran away very quickly while we remained pinned there under the blazing sun, with Raymond holding his arm dripping with blood.

Masson immediately told us there was a doctor up on the ridge who spent every Sunday there. Raymond wanted to go to him right away. Every time he tried to speak, blood from the gash in his mouth formed little bubbles. We held him up and went back to the house as quickly as possible. When we got there, Raymond said that his injuries were superficial but that he would go to see the doctor. He left with Masson and I stayed behind with the women to explain what had happened. Masson's wife started crying and Marie went very pale. I found it annoying to have to explain everything to them. In the end, I didn't say anything else and smoked a cigarette while watching the sea.

At about one-thirty, Raymond came back with Masson. His arm was bandaged and he had a patch over the corner of his mouth. The doctor had told him it was nothing but Raymond looked very gloomy. Masson tried to make him laugh but he refused to say anything. When he said he was going down to the beach, I asked him where he was headed. He replied that he wanted to get some air. Masson and I said we'd go with him. Then he got angry and swore at us. Masson said it was best not to upset him. But I . . . I followed him anyway.

We walked along the beach for a long while. The sun was now scorching hot. Its light crashed down, shattering over the sand and the sea. I got the impression that Raymond knew where he was going, but I was probably wrong. At the very end of the beach, we came to a little spring that flowed down into the sand from behind a large rock. It was there that we came upon our two Arabs. They were stretched out in their sweaty blue work clothes. They looked quite calm and almost pleased. They didn't seem to notice us and their expression never changed. The one who'd attacked Raymond looked at him in silence. The other one was blowing into a little flute, playing the same three notes he could get out of it over and over again while watching us from out of the corner of his eye.

All this time there was nothing but the sun and the silence, broken only by the soft sound of the flowing water and the three musical notes. Then Raymond took a gun out of his pocket, but the Arab didn't move and they just kept watching each other. I noticed that the one playing the flute had spread his toes out very wide. Then, without taking his eyes off his enemy, Raymond asked: 'Should I kill him?' I thought that if I said no, he'd get all worked up and would certainly fire. So all I said was: 'He hasn't said anything to you yet. It wouldn't be right to just shoot him like that.' We could still hear the soft sound of the water and the flute amid the sun and the deep silence. Then Raymond said: 'All right then; I'll swear at him and when he answers back, I'll shoot him.' I replied: 'Right. But if he doesn't take out his knife, you can't shoot.' Raymond started getting all worked up. The other Arab kept on playing his flute and both of them were staring at us, watching Raymond's every movement. 'No,' I said to Raymond. 'Take him on man to man and give me your gun. If the other one joins in or he pulls out his knife, I'll shoot him.'

When Raymond gave me his gun, the sun flashed off it. We stood dead still, as if everything were closing in around us. We were staring at each other and everything stopped dead, caught between the sea, the sand and the sun, the double silence of the flute and the water. At that very moment, I thought that I could either fire or not fire. But suddenly, the Arabs backed away from us and hid behind the rock. So Raymond and I headed back. Raymond seemed to feel better and talked about which bus we'd get home.

I walked back to the beach house with him, and while he went up the wooden stairs, I stopped at the first step, my head throbbing from the sun, put off by the effort it would take to climb the wooden staircase and deal with the women again. But the heat was so intense that it hurt to stand motionless beneath the blinding sun that rained down from the sky. Whether I stayed or went made no difference.

A moment later, I turned back towards the beach and started walking.

I felt the same dazzling explosion of blazing sun. The sea, gasping for breath, sent rapid little waves to wash over the sand. I walked slowly towards the rocks and I could feel my forehead swelling up beneath the sun. The intense heat beat down on me, as if trying to force me back. And every time I felt its hot blast against my face, I clenched my teeth, tightened my fists in my pockets, strained with all my being to triumph over the sun and the dizzying fire it unleashed upon me. My jaw tensed tightly every time a piercing ray of light shot up from the sand, a white seashell or a piece of broken glass. I walked for a long time.

I could see the dark little shape of the rock in the distance surrounded by a blinding halo of light and spray from the sea. I thought about the cool water behind the rock. I wanted to return to the soft sound of the water, wanted to escape the sun, the strain, the women's tears, wanted to find peace once more in the shade. But when I got closer, I saw that Raymond's Arab had come back.

He was alone. He was stretched out on his back, his hands under his neck, his forehead hidden by the shadows cast by the rock, his whole body bathed in sunlight. His overalls were steaming from the heat. I was a little surprised. As far as I was concerned, the matter was closed and I'd ended up here by chance.

As soon as he saw me, he raised himself up a bit and put his hand in his pocket. I instinctively felt for Raymond's gun. Then he leaned back again, but he kept his hand in his pocket. I was quite far away from him, about ten metres or so. I could see him looking at me every now and then, his eyes half closed. But most of the time his face seemed to flicker before me in the fiery air. The sound of the waves was even more languorous, calmer than at midday. It was the same relentless sun, the same light on the same sand. For two hours now, the sun had hovered in the sky, two hours since it had cast anchor in an ocean of molten metal. On the horizon, a small steamship passed by and I could see its dark smudge out of the corner of my eye, for I never stopped watching the Arab.

I thought that all I had to do was turn around and walk away and it would all be over. But an entire beach pulsating with sun pressed me to go on. I took a few steps towards the spring. The Arab hadn't moved. He was actually still quite far away. Perhaps because of the way his face was hidden in shadow he seemed to be laughing. I waited. The burning sun struck my cheeks and I could feel drops of sweat gathering above my eyebrows. It was the same sun as the day I'd buried Mama, and like then it was my forehead that hurt the most and I could feel every vein throbbing beneath my skin. I was being burned alive; I couldn't stand it any more so I took a step forward. I knew it was stupid; I knew I couldn't shake off the sun simply by taking one step. But I took that step, one single step forward. And this time, without getting up, the Arab pulled out his knife and raised it towards me in the sun. The light flashed off the steel and it was as if a long gleaming blade was thrust deep into my forehead. At that very moment, the sweat that had gathered on my eyebrows suddenly rushed down into my eyes, blinding me with a warm, heavy veil of salt and tears. All I could feel was the sun crashing like cymbals against my forehead, and the knife, a burning sword hovering above me.

Its red-hot blade tore through my eyelashes to pierce my aching eyes. It was then that everything started to sway. The sea heaved a heavy, scorching sigh. The sky seemed to split apart from end to end to pour its fire down upon me. My whole body tensed as I gripped the gun more tightly. It set off the trigger. I could feel the smooth barrel in my hand and it was then, with that sharp, deafening sound, that it all began. I shook off the sweat and the sun. I realized that I had destroyed the natural balance of the day, the exceptional silence of a beach where I had once been happy. Then I fired four more times into the lifeless body, where the bullets sank without leaving a trace. And it was as if I had rapped sharply, four times, on the fatal door of destiny.

*Part Two*

# 1

Immediately after my arrest, I was interrogated several times. But they were just preliminary questions about my identity and didn't last very long. That first time at the police station no one seemed interested in my case. A week later, however, the judge in charge of the investigation on behalf of the prosecution looked at me with curiosity. But to start with, he only asked for my name and address, my profession, date of birth and where I was born. Then he wanted to know if I had a lawyer. I said I didn't and asked if it was absolutely necessary. 'Why?' he said. I replied that I found my case very simple. He smiled and said: 'That's one way of looking at it. But the law is clear. If you don't have a lawyer, the court will assign you one.' I thought it was very convenient that the legal system took responsibility for such details and told him so. He agreed with me and said he felt the law was well thought out.

In the beginning, I didn't take him seriously. He interviewed me in a room with curtains at the windows; there was a small lamp on his desk that shone on the armchair where I had to sit while he remained in the darkness. I'd read scenes in books just like this and it all seemed like a game to me. After our conversation, however, I really looked at him: I saw a tall man with delicate features, deep blue eyes, a long grey moustache and a thick head of hair that was almost completely white. He came across as very reasonable and actually quite kind, in spite of a nervous twitch at the corner of his mouth. When I was leaving, I was even going to stretch out my hand to shake his, but I remembered just in time that I'd killed a man.

The next day, a lawyer came to see me in prison. He was short and chubby, rather young, and his hair was carefully slicked back. In spite of the heat (I was in shirtsleeves), he was wearing a dark suit, a wing collar and a strange-looking tie with wide black-and-white stripes. He put the briefcase he was carrying under his arm down on my bed, introduced himself and told me he had studied my file. My case was a tricky one but he was sure we could win if I put my trust in him. I thanked him and he said: 'Let's get down to business.'

He sat on the bed and explained they had obtained certain information about my private life. They'd found out that my mother had recently died at an old people's home. So they had made enquiries in Marengo. The prosecution had learned that 'I'd shown no emotion' on the day of Mama's funeral. 'I'm sorry to have to ask you about this,' my lawyer said, 'but it's very important. And it will be a key argument for the prosecution if I have nothing to counter it.' He wanted me to help him. He asked me if I'd been upset that day. I found the question quite surprising and thought how embarrassed I would have been if I'd had to ask it. Nevertheless, I replied that I'd rather lost the habit of analysing my emotions and so it was difficult to explain. I undoubtedly loved Mama very much, but that didn't mean anything. Every normal person sometimes wishes the people they love would die. When I said that, the lawyer cut in and seemed really disturbed. He made me promise not to say that in court or to the judge handling my interrogation. Then I explained that one of the characteristics of my personality was that physical sensations often got in the way of my emotions. The day of Mama's funeral, I was very tired and sleepy. So much so that I wasn't really aware of what was happening. Though I could definitely say that I would have preferred it if Mama hadn't died. But my lawyer didn't seem pleased. 'That's not good enough,' he said.

He thought for a moment. Then he asked if he could say I had kept my emotions under control that day. I said: 'No, because it isn't true.' He looked at me strangely, as if I disgusted him slightly. He told me, rather maliciously, that in any case the director and staff of the home would be called as witnesses and that 'things could turn very nasty for me'. I pointed out that this other business had nothing to do with my case, but he simply replied that it was obvious I'd never had any dealings with the judicial system.

He left looking angry. I would have liked to call him back, explain to him that I wanted his sympathy – not so that he would defend me better, but because it was natural to feel that way, so to speak. I especially noticed that I made him feel uncomfortable. He didn't understand me and seemed a little resentful towards me. I wanted to tell him that I was just like everybody else, exactly like everybody else. But when all was said and done, there wasn't much point so I didn't bother because it just seemed like too much trouble.

A little while later, I was once again taken down to be questioned by the judge. It was two o'clock in the afternoon and this time his office was flooded with light because the sheer curtains at the windows barely blocked it out. It was very hot. He very politely asked me to sit down and said that my lawyer couldn't be there 'due to unforeseen circumstances'. But I had the right not to answer his questions and to wait until my lawyer could assist me. I said I could answer his questions on my own. He pressed a buzzer on his desk. A young clerk came in and sat down really close behind me.

We both settled back in our chairs. The interrogation began. The first thing he told me was that I was being depicted as taciturn and uncommunicative and he wanted to know my reaction to that. I replied: 'It's just that I don't ever have much to say, so I keep quiet.' He smiled as he had the first time, admitted that that was the best reason and added: 'In any case, that's of no importance.' He fell silent, looked at me, then sat up very tall and quite suddenly said: 'What interests me is you.' I didn't really know what he meant by that and I didn't reply. 'There are certain things about what you did that I can't comprehend,' he added. 'I'm sure you'll help me to understand.' I said that it was very simple. He encouraged me to go over what I'd done that day. I told him everything I'd already gone over: Raymond, the beach, swimming, the fight, the beach again, the little spring, the sun and the five shots I'd fired. He kept saying: 'Fine, fine' while I was talking. When I got to the part where the body was stretched out, he nodded in approval and said: 'Good.' But I was tired of telling the same story over and over again and felt like I'd never talked so much.

After a moment's silence, he stood up and said he wanted to help me; he found me interesting and, with God's help, he could do something for me. But first he wanted to ask me a few more questions. Without pausing, he asked me if

I loved Mama. I said: 'Yes, like everyone else', and the clerk, who up to that point had been typing at a steady pace, must have made a mistake because he stopped and had to go back and correct it. Then, for no apparent reason, the judge again asked if I'd fired the five shots all in a row. I thought about it and explained I'd fired once and then, after a few seconds, the next four shots. 'Why did you wait between the first and second shots?' he asked. Once more I could see the burning beach and feel the scorching sun beating down on my forehead. But this time, I didn't reply. During the entire silence that followed, the judge seemed to be getting all worked up. He sat down, ran his fingers through his hair, put his elbows on the desk and finally leaned in towards me with a strange expression on his face: 'Why, *why* did you fire at a man who was already dead?' Again, I didn't know what to say. The judge wiped his forehead and repeated his question in a slightly different tone of voice: '*Why*? I *insist* that you tell me. *Why*?' I remained silent.

Suddenly, he got up, strode over to the other end of his office and opened a drawer of his filing cabinet. He took out a silver crucifix and brandished it at me as he came closer. And in a completely different voice, almost quivering, he shouted: 'Do you know who this is?' I said: 'Yes, of course.' Then, speaking very quickly and passionately, he told me that he believed in God, that he was positive that no man was so guilty that God could not forgive him, but that in order to be forgiven the man must repent and once more become a child whose soul is bare and prepared to accept everything. His entire body was leaning towards me over the table. He was waving his crucifix almost directly above me. To tell the truth, I had great difficulty in following his reasoning, first of all because I was hot and there were some big flies in his office that kept landing on my face and also because he scared me a little. At the same time, though, I realized this was ridiculous because, after all, I was the one who was the criminal. But he kept on going. I vaguely understood that in his opinion there was only one puzzling thing in my confession: the fact that I'd waited before firing the second shot. He was quite happy with all the rest, but that, he just couldn't comprehend.

I started to tell him he was wrong to keep going on about this: it simply wasn't that important. But he cut me off, drew himself up to his full height and demanded I tell him one last time if I believed in God. I said no. He sat down, looking indignant. He said that was impossible, that everyone believed in God, even those who turned away from Him. This was his firm belief, and if he ever had cause to doubt it, his life would no longer have any meaning. 'Do you want my life to have no meaning?' he shouted. In my opinion, that was none of my business and I told him so. But from across the table, he was already thrusting the Christ figure in my face and screaming like a madman: '*I* am a Christian! I ask Christ to forgive your sins! How can you not believe that He suffered for you?' It struck me that he was now addressing me in a very personal way, as if I were a child, but I'd had enough. It was getting hotter and hotter. As always, whenever I want to get rid of people I'm barely listening to, I try to look as if I'm agreeing with them. To my surprise, he sounded triumphant: 'You see, you see,' he said. 'You do believe, don't you, and you will put your trust in Him?' Obviously, I said no again. He slumped back into his chair.

He looked very tired. He sat there in silence for a moment while the typist, who had been taking down the entire conversation, finished off the last few sentences. Then he looked at me intently and rather sadly. 'I've never met anyone with such a hardened soul as yours,' he said softly. 'Every criminal who has stood before me has always cried when faced with this symbol of suffering.' I was about to reply that that was because they were criminals. But then I realized I was also a criminal; it was an idea I was having trouble coming to terms with. The judge stood up as if to indicate that the interrogation was over. All he asked me then, in the same slightly weary tone of voice, was whether I regretted what I'd done. I thought about it and replied that rather than feeling genuine regret I found it all rather tedious. I had the impression that he didn't understand me. But nothing more happened that day.

During the days that followed, I saw the examining judge often. On each occasion, though, my lawyer was present. The questions were limited to asking me details about certain points in my previous statements. Or sometimes the judge discussed the charges with my lawyer. But, to tell the truth, they never took any notice of me during these meetings. Gradually, however, the tone of the interrogations changed. It seemed as if the judge were no longer interested in me and saw my case as more or less closed. He didn't talk to me about God any more and I never saw him get as worked up as on that first day. As a result, our meetings became more cordial. After a few questions and a bit of discussion with my lawyer, the interrogation was over. My case was progressing, as the judge put it. Sometimes, when the conversation dealt with general matters, I was even included. I started to be able to breathe freely again. During these meetings, no one was unkind to me. Everything was so natural, so well organized and so seriously played out that I had the ridiculous impression that I was 'one of the family'. And throughout the entire eleven months of the investigation, I can honestly say that I was almost surprised to realize that the only moments I had ever really enjoyed were the rare times when the judge would walk me back to the door of his office, pat me on the shoulder and say in a friendly tone of voice: 'That's all for our Antichrist today.' Then I'd be handed back to the guards.

## 2

There are certain things I've never liked talking about. I realized after my first few days in prison that I wouldn't like to talk about that part of my life.

Later on such things no longer bothered me: they weren't important. To tell the truth, I wasn't really in prison the first few days: I was just vaguely waiting for something new to happen. It was only after the first and only time Marie visited me that everything began. From the day I received her letter (she told me they wouldn't let her come because she wasn't my wife), from that day on, I felt as if my cell was my home and that my life would end there. The day I was arrested, I was locked up in a room with several prisoners, most of them Arabs. They laughed when they saw me. They asked me what I'd done. I said I'd killed an Arab and they all went quiet. But a short time later, night fell. They showed me how to set up the mat where I would sleep. By rolling up one of the ends, you could make a sort of pillow. Bugs crawled across my face all night long. A few days later, I was put in a cell by myself where I slept on a wooden bed. I had a bucket for a toilet and a metal washbowl. The prison was right at the top of the town and I could see the sea through a little window. One day, I was holding on to the bars of the window, my face raised towards the sun, when a guard came in and told me I had a visitor. I thought it must be Marie. I was right.

To get to the visitors' area, I walked down a long corridor, then up a flight of stairs and finally down another corridor. I went into a very large, very bright room lit by an enormous bay window. The room was divided into three sections by two large sets of bars that ran down it lengthwise. Between the two sets of bars there was a gap of eight to ten metres that separated the prisoners from the visitors. I saw Marie sitting opposite me; her face was tanned and she was wearing her striped dress. There were ten prisoners or so on my side, most of them Arabs. Marie was surrounded by Arab women and sat between two other visitors: a little old woman with pursed lips dressed all in black and a bare-headed fat woman who spoke very loudly while making lots of gestures. Because of the distance between them, the visitors and the prisoners had to talk very loudly. When I first came in, I felt rather dizzy because of the blaring voices echoing between the large bare walls of the room and the blinding sunlight pouring in through the windows. My cell was quieter and darker. It took me a few seconds to adjust. But then I could see each face clearly, outlined against the bright daylight. I noticed that a guard was sitting at the end of the corridor between the two sets of bars. Most of the Arab prisoners and their families sat on the floor, facing each other. They weren't shouting. In spite of all the commotion, they managed to hear each other even though they spoke very quietly. Their muffled whispers, rising from below, created a kind of soft background music against the conversations that criss-crossed above their heads. I noticed all this very quickly as I walked towards Marie. She was already leaning against the bars and smiling at me as brightly as she could. I thought she looked very beautiful, but I didn't know how to tell her.

'Well,' she said very loudly. 'So here we are. Are you all right? Do you have everything you need?' 'Yes, everything.'

We fell silent and Marie kept on smiling. The fat woman was shouting at the man next to me, her husband presumably – a big, light-skinned man with an honest face. She was continuing a conversation they'd already started.

'Jeanne didn't want to take him!' she shouted at the top of her lungs. 'Right,' the man said, 'right.' 'I told her you'd have him back when you got out, but she didn't want to take him.'

Marie shouted that Raymond said hello and I replied: 'Thanks.' But my voice was blocked out by the man next to me who was asking 'if he was all right'. His wife laughed and said: 'Never better.' The prisoner to my left, a small young man with delicate hands, never spoke. I noticed he was sitting opposite the little old woman and that the two of them were staring at each other intently. But I didn't have time to watch them any more because Marie shouted that I shouldn't give up hope. I said: 'Yes.' I looked at her and wanted to touch her shoulder. I wanted to feel the soft fabric of her dress and didn't exactly know what else I could hope for. But that was surely what Marie must have meant because she kept smiling. All I could see were her bright teeth and the little wrinkles around her eyes. 'You'll get out and we'll get married!' she shouted again. 'Do you think so?' I replied, mainly because I had to say something. Then she said very quickly and still very loudly that of course I would be acquitted and we'd be able to go swimming again.

But the woman beside her was shouting, saying she'd left a basket of food at the clerk's office. She listed all the things she'd put in it. It had to be checked because everything was so expensive. The prisoner next to me and his mother were still watching each other. The murmuring of the Arabs continued beneath us. Outside, the light seemed to intensify against the bay window.

I felt slightly sick and wanted to leave. The noise was painful. But on the other hand, I wanted to be with Marie for as long as I could. I don't know how much time passed. Marie told me about her work and never stopped smiling. The murmuring, the shouting, the conversations continued all around me. The only oasis of silence was the small young man and the elderly woman next to me who sat silently looking at each other. Gradually, the Arabs were led out. Almost everyone stopped talking as soon as the first one left. The little old woman moved closer to the bars just as the guard gestured to her son. He said: 'Goodbye, Mama' and she slipped her hand between the bars, letting it linger there in a sad little wave goodbye.

She left just as a man holding a hat in his hand came in to take her place. Another prisoner was brought in and the two men started talking excitedly, but whispering softly, because the room had gone quiet again. They came to take away the man to my right; his wife said quite loudly, as if she hadn't realized she no longer needed to shout: 'Take good care of yourself, and be careful.' Then it was my turn. Marie blew me a kiss. I turned around and looked back before going inside. She didn't move, her face crushed against the bars with the same tense, distressed smile.

Soon afterwards, she wrote to me. And that was when the

things I never liked to talk about began. I shouldn't really complain, though, because it was easier for me than for some of the others. At the beginning of my imprisonment, however, what I found most difficult was that I had the thoughts of a free man. For example, I was obsessed by a desire to be on a beach and to walk down to the sea. When I imagined the sound of those first little waves beneath my feet, the sensation of water flowing over my body and the feeling of freedom this brought me, it struck me how much the walls of my prison had closed in on me. But that just lasted a few months. Afterwards, I had only the thoughts of a prisoner. I looked forward to the daily walk I took around the courtyard or the visit from my lawyer. As for the rest of the time, I got used to it. I often thought that if I'd been forced to live inside the hollow trunk of a dead tree, with nothing to do except look up at the sky flowering above my head, I would have eventually got used to that as well. I would have looked forward to the birds flying by or the clouds drifting into one another, just as I looked forward to seeing the odd ties my lawyer wore, just as in another time and place, I'd waited eagerly for Saturdays so I could press Marie's body close to mine. Although, when I really thought about it, I wasn't living in a dead tree. There were people who were worse off than me. It was an idea of Mama's that people could eventually get used to anything, and she often talked about it.

Most of the time, I didn't think about things much at all. The first months were difficult. But because of that, the effort I had to make helped pass the time. For example, I was tormented by the desire to have a woman. It was natural, I was young. I never specifically thought about Marie.

But I thought so much about a woman – women, about all the women I'd known, all the circumstances in which I'd made love to them – that I could feel their living presence in my prison cell, their faces arousing my desire. In one respect, it upset me, but in another way, it killed the time. I'd managed to win over the head guard who accompanied the kitchen boy when he brought my meals. He was the one who first talked to me about women. He told me it was the first thing everyone complained about. I told him I felt the same and that I found it unfair to be treated like this. 'But that's exactly why they put people in prison,' he said. 'What do you mean?' 'That's what freedom is, you see. They're taking away your freedom.' I'd never thought of that. I agreed with him. 'It's true,' I said, 'otherwise what would be the punishment?' 'That's right; at least you understand how things are. The others don't. But they all end up finding ways to relieve their frustrations.' Then the guard left.

There was also the issue of cigarettes. When I first went to prison, they took away my belt, my shoelaces, my tie and everything in my pockets, including my cigarettes. Once inside my cell, I asked for them back. But I was told it wasn't allowed. The first few days were really rough. That got to me the most. I used to suck on bits of wood I'd pulled off the boards from my bed. All day long, I felt constantly nauseous. I couldn't understand why they wouldn't let me have something that didn't do any harm to anyone else. Later on I understood that it was also part of the punishment. But by then I'd got used to not smoking any more, so it was no longer a punishment to me.

Apart from those few problems, I wasn't too unhappy. Once again, it was all a matter of how to kill time. I finally stopped being bored altogether from the moment I learned how to remember. Sometimes I started thinking about my bedroom and I would imagine starting at one end of it and walking around in a circle while mentally listing all the things I passed. At the beginning, it took no time at all. But every time I started doing it again, it took a little longer because I would remember all the different pieces of furniture, every object on the furniture, every detail of each object, their colour and texture, and any marks, cracks or chips. At the same time, I tried to concentrate so I would have a complete inventory. I became such an expert at this that by the end of a few weeks I could spend hours simply listing everything in my bedroom. The more I thought about it, the more things came back to me, things I hadn't noticed before or had forgotten. I realized then that a man who had only lived for a single day could easily live a hundred years in prison. He would have enough memories to keep him from getting bored. In one respect, it was an advantage.

Then there was sleep. In the beginning, I slept badly at night and not at all during the day. Little by little, my nights got better and I could also sleep during the day. In the last months, I would say that I slept between sixteen and eighteen hours a day. That left me six hours to kill with meals, my basic needs, my memories and the story of the man from Czechoslovakia.

Between my mattress and the wooden bed, I'd found a worn scrap of newspaper, yellow with age; it was almost completely stuck to the mattress. The beginning of the article was missing, but it was a story about something that must have happened in Czechoslovakia.

A man left a Czech village to make his fortune. Twenty-five years later, he was rich and returned to the village with his wife and child. His mother ran a hotel with his sister in the town where he was born. To surprise them, he'd left his wife and child in another hotel and gone to his mother's; she didn't recognize him when he came in. As a joke, he had the idea of taking a room. He'd let them see his money. During the night, his mother and sister murdered him, to rob him, beating him to death with a hammer and throwing his body into the river. In the morning, his wife arrived and not knowing what had happened revealed the identity of the traveller. The mother hanged herself. The sister threw herself down a well. I must have read this story thousands of times. In one sense, it was highly improbable. In another way, it was plausible. In any case, I felt that the traveller had sort of deserved what he got, because you should never joke around like that.

So between the hours spent sleeping, remembering things, reading my story and watching the light fade into darkness and then grow light again, the time passed. I'd read somewhere that people ended up losing their notion of time in prison. But that made little sense to me. I didn't understand how the days could be so long and yet so short. Long to get through, of course, but so distended that they ended up running into each other, so the names of the days of the week got lost. 'Yesterday' and 'tomorrow' were the only words that meant anything to me.

One day, when the guard told me I'd been there for five months, I believed him but I couldn't understand it. To me, the same day had endlessly played itself out in my cell and I'd set myself the same goal each time. That day, after the guard had gone, I looked at myself in my metal dish. It seemed as if my reflection remained grave even when I tried to smile at it. I moved it about in front of me. I was smiling but my face still had the same sad, harsh expression. The day was ending and the hour was approaching that I don't want to talk about, that nameless time when the sounds of the night rise up throughout the entire prison, accompanied by a cortège of silence. I walked over to the small window and studied my reflection once more in the fading light. My face still looked serious, but why should that be surprising when at that very moment I was serious as well? At the same time, though, and for the first time in months, I could clearly hear the sound of my own voice. I recognized it as the voice that had resonated in my ears throughout all those long days, and I realized I had been talking to myself. I recalled then what the nurse had said at Mama's funeral. No, there was no way out, and no one can imagine what the nights are like in prison.

# 3

I can honestly say that one summer quickly followed the next. As the first warm days approached, I sensed that something new was awaiting me. My case was due to be heard in the last session of the Crown Court, which finished at the end of June. The proceedings opened with the sun blazing outside the courtroom. My lawyer had assured me that it wouldn't last more than two or three days. 'And besides,' he added, 'the judge will be in a hurry because your case isn't the most important one of the session. There's a parricide scheduled right after you.'

At seven-thirty in the morning, someone came to get me and the police van took me to the courthouse. The two policemen showed me into a small room that smelled musty. We waited, sitting next to a door; on the other side, we could hear voices, names being called out, the scraping of chairs and the kind of commotion that made me think of certain local celebrations when the furniture in a room is rearranged after a concert so everyone can dance. The policemen told me we had to wait to be called into the courtroom and one of them offered me a cigarette, which I refused. A little while later he asked me if 'I was nervous'. I said no and that, in a way, I was quite interested in seeing a trial. I'd never been to one before. 'Yes,' said the second policeman, 'but in the end it tires you out.'

After a while, a little bell rang in the room. They took off my handcuffs. They opened the door and led me into the dock. The room was jam-packed. In spite of the blinds, the sun filtered through in places and it was already stifling hot. They'd left the windows closed. I sat down and the policemen stood on either side of me. It was then that I noticed a row of faces in front of me. They were all watching me: I realized they were the jury. But they all looked the same to me. I had only one impression: I was standing in front of a row of seats on a tram and all the anonymous passengers were looking up and down at the person who had just got on, to see what was contemptible about him. I knew very well that it was a silly thought because no one here was trying to see what was contemptible; they were trying to see if I looked like a criminal. But there's not much difference between the two things, and in any case, that was what I thought at the time.

I was also a little confused by all the people crammed into this confined space. I looked around again and couldn't make out a single face. I don't believe it had even occurred to me at first that all these people were eager to get a look at me. No one normally took any notice of me. It took some effort on my part to understand that I was the cause of all this commotion. 'There are so many people!' I said to the policeman. He told me it was because of the newspapers, then pointed to a group of journalists near a table beneath the jury box. 'There they are,' he said. I asked: 'Who?' and he replied: 'The journalists.' He knew one of them; the man spotted him and started walking towards us. He was middle-aged, kind-looking and grimaced slightly. He shook the policeman's hand very warmly. I noticed that everyone was talking in little groups, calling out to one another, chatting, like in a club where everyone is happy to find other people from the same social set. I also couldn't explain the bizarre impression I had of being superfluous, a little as if I were an intruder. Nevertheless, the journalist spoke to me and smiled. He said he hoped it would all go well for me. I thanked him and he added: 'You know, we've written a small piece about your case. Summer is the slow season for newspapers. Only your story and the parricide were of any interest.' Then he pointed out a small gentleman who was standing with the group he'd just left; he was wearing enormous glasses with black rims and looked like a fat weasel. He told me the man was a special correspondent from a Parisian newspaper: 'He didn't come for your case, though. But since he's meant to report on the parricide, they asked him to send in your story at the same time.' I was about to thank him again but I thought that would be ridiculous. He gave me a friendly little wave and walked away. We waited a few more minutes.

My lawyer arrived wearing his robe and surrounded by several of his colleagues. He went over to the journalists and shook their hands. They exchanged pleasantries, laughing and seeming completely at ease, right until the moment the bell rang in the courtroom. Everyone took his place. My lawyer came over to me, shook my hand and advised me to reply as briefly as possible to the questions I was asked, not to offer any additional information and to count on him to do the rest.

To my left, I heard the sound of a chair being moved and I saw a tall, thin man, dressed all in red, with a pince-nez; he sat down, carefully folding his robe under him. It was the prosecutor. A clerk announced that the court was in session. At that very moment, two large fans began to whirr. Three judges, two of them in black and the third in red, came into the courtroom with their files and very quickly took their places on the high platform. The man in the red robe sat in the chair in the middle, placed his cap on the table in front of him, wiped his small, bald head with a handkerchief and declared the proceedings officially open.

The journalists already had their pens in their hands. They all had the same indifferent, slightly mocking expression on their faces. With the exception of one of them, much younger than the others, dressed in grey flannel and wearing a blue tie; he had left his pen on the table in front of him and was staring at me. On his vaguely asymmetrical face, all I could see were his very bright eyes examining me attentively, yet without expressing anything I could put my finger on. And I had the bizarre impression of being watched by myself. It was perhaps because of this, and also because I didn't understand the court procedures, that I didn't really take in everything that happened next: the way the jurors were selected, the questions the presiding judge asked my lawyer, the prosecutor and the jury (all the jurors' heads would turn towards the judges at the same time), a quick reading out of the official charges, which contained the names of people and places I recognized, and some additional questions to my lawyer.

Then the presiding judge said we should move on to calling the witnesses. The clerk read out several names that caught my attention. From amid the crowd of spectators I had seen only as a shapeless mass, I watched as each person stood up, one by one, and went out by a side door: the director and caretaker from the old people's home, the elderly Thomas Pérez, Raymond, Masson, Salamano, Marie. She gave me a nervous little wave. I was surprised I hadn't noticed them earlier but then the final witness, Céleste, stood up when his name was called. Beside him, I recognized the little woman from the restaurant; she was wearing a jacket and had the same precise manner and purposeful look. She was staring at me intently. But I didn't have time to think about it because the presiding judge began to speak. He said that the official proceedings were about to begin and that he knew he didn't have to remind the members of the public that they were to remain orderly. He felt that his role was to preside over the trial with impartiality and to consider the case objectively. The jury's sentence would be made in the spirit of justice and, in any case, he would clear the courtroom if given the slightest reason to do so.

It was getting hotter and I could see the spectators fanning themselves with newspapers. There was a constant rustling of paper. The presiding judge gestured to the clerk, who brought in three straw fans that the judges started using immediately.

My interrogation began at once. The presiding judge questioned me calmly and even, or so it seemed to me, with a touch of cordiality. Once again I was asked to confirm my identity, and in spite of my irritation I thought that, actually, all this was only natural because it would be a very serious matter to pass judgement on somebody mistaking him for someone else. Then the presiding judge began explaining what I had done, stopping every three sentences to turn to me and ask: 'Is that correct?' Each time I replied: 'Yes, your Honour', as my lawyer had instructed me to do. It took a long time because the presiding judge had included in his account every minute detail of what had happened. The whole time he was speaking, the journalists took notes. I could feel the youngest one and the little robotic woman watching me. The members of the jury – all those passengers on the tram – were looking at the presiding judge, who coughed, leafed through his file and turned towards me while fanning himself.

He then told me he had to ask some questions which might seem unconnected to my case, but which could perhaps have significant bearing on it. I realized he was going to talk about Mama again and immediately felt very uncomfortable. He asked me why I had put Mama in the home. I replied that it was because I didn't have enough money to look after her or to pay for someone else to take care of her. He asked me if that had affected me personally and I replied that neither Mama nor I expected anything of each other, nor from anyone else for that matter, and that we had both got used to our new lives. The presiding judge then said that he didn't want to dwell on that point and asked the prosecutor if he had any questions for me.

The prosecutor half turned his back on me and, without looking at me, stated that with the permission of the presiding judge, he would like to know if I had gone back to the little spring alone with the intention of killing the Arab. I said: 'No.' 'In that case, why was he armed, and why go back to that precise spot?' I said that it was by chance. Then the prosecutor added in a rather unpleasant way: 'That will be all for now.' Everything then got rather confusing, at least to me. But after consulting with several people, the presiding judge announced that court was adjourned and would reconvene that afternoon to hear the witnesses.

I didn't have time to think about anything. They took me away, put me into a police van and we went back to the prison, where I had lunch. After a very short time, just long enough for me to realize I was tired, they came back for me; everything started over again and I found myself in the same courtroom, in front of the same faces as before. Only this time it was much hotter and, as if by some miracle, each member of the jury, along with the prosecutor, my lawyer and some of the journalists, now had straw fans. The young journalist and the little woman were still there. But they weren't fanning themselves; they just kept watching me without saying a word.

I wiped the sweat from my face and only became aware of where I was and what was happening to me when I heard the director of the old people's home called to the witness box. He was asked if Mama ever complained about me and he said yes, but that it was rather an obsession of the residents to complain about their relatives. The presiding judge asked him if she specifically blamed me for having put her in the home and the director said yes again. But this time he didn't add anything. To another question, he replied that he'd been surprised at how calm I was on the day of the funeral. He was asked what he meant by 'calm'. The director then looked down at his shoes and said that I hadn't wanted to see Mama, I hadn't cried once and I'd left as soon as the funeral was over without spending any time at the graveside. Another thing had surprised him: one of the employees from the funeral home had told him I didn't know how old Mama was. There was a moment of silence and the presiding judge asked him to confirm he was actually talking about me. Since the director didn't understand the question, he explained: 'It's the law.' Then the presiding judge asked the prosecutor if he had any questions to ask of the witness and the prosecutor shouted: 'Oh no, that will do nicely!' with such intensity and a look of triumph in my direction that for the first time in many years I felt a ridiculous desire to cry, because I could sense how much all these people hated me.

After asking the jury and my lawyer if they had any questions, the presiding judge heard the caretaker's testimony. The same formalities were repeated for him as for all the others. When he came in, the caretaker glanced over at me and then looked away. He answered the questions put to him. He said that I hadn't wanted to see Mama, that I'd smoked a cigarette, fallen asleep and drunk some coffee. I then felt some sort of indignation filling the courtroom and, for the first time, I realized I was guilty. They asked the caretaker to repeat what he'd said about the cigarette and the coffee. The prosecutor looked at me with a sarcastic gleam in his eyes. Then my lawyer asked the caretaker if he had smoked a cigarette with me as well. But the prosecutor angrily stood up to object to the question: 'Who is the criminal in this matter and why should such methods be employed to tarnish the State's witnesses in order to play down the importance of their testimony, testimony which remains damning, nonetheless!' The presiding judge instructed the caretaker to answer the question. The old man said in an embarrassed voice: 'I know I was wrong to do it. But I didn't dare refuse the cigarette the gentleman offered me.' Finally, I was asked if I had anything I wanted to add. 'Nothing,' I replied, 'except that the witness is right. It's true that I offered him a cigarette.' The caretaker then looked at me with some surprise and with a kind of gratitude. He hesitated, then said that he was the one who had offered to give me some coffee. My lawyer loudly and triumphantly declared that the members of the jury would take into account what had been said. But the prosecutor shouted above our heads, saying: 'Yes, the Gentlemen of the Jury will indeed take it into account. And they will come to the conclusion that a stranger might offer a coffee, but that a son should refuse it when in the presence of the dead body of the woman who brought him into this world.' The caretaker went back to his seat.

When it was Thomas Pérez's turn, a clerk had to help him into the witness box. Pérez said he had known my mother particularly well and that he had only seen me once, on the day of the funeral. He was asked what I had done that day and he replied: 'You know, I was very distraught myself. So I didn't notice anything. I was suffering so much that I didn't notice a thing. Because for me, it was a horrible loss. I even fainted. So I didn't really see the gentleman.' The prosecutor asked him if he had at least seen me cry. Pérez said no. Then the prosecutor said: 'The Gentlemen of the Jury will take that into account.' But my lawyer got angry. In a tone of voice that seemed rather melodramatic to me, he asked Pérez 'if he had seen that I wasn't crying'. Pérez said: 'No.' The spectators laughed. And my lawyer, rolling back one of his sleeves, said emphatically: 'So this is what this

trial has come to. Everything is true and nothing is true!'
The prosecutor looked impassive and tapped his pencil on
the covers of his files.

There was a break of five minutes; my lawyer told me
everything was going well. Then we heard Céleste's testimony; he was called as a witness for the defence. The
defence – that was me. Céleste glanced over at me every
now and then while fiddling with his panama hat. He had
on the new suit he wore whenever we went to the races
together on a Sunday. But it looked as though he hadn't
managed to put on his detachable collar because only a collar stud was holding his shirt closed. They asked him if I
was one of his clients and he said: 'Yes, but he's also a friend';
then what he thought of me and he replied that I was a man;
then what he meant by that and he replied that everyone
knew what that meant. Next they asked if I was uncommunicative, but he just replied that I didn't say anything if I
had nothing to say. The prosecutor asked him if I normally
paid my rent on time. Céleste laughed and said: 'That's
between us.' Then they asked him what he thought about
my crime. He clenched his hands around the edge of the
witness box and you could tell he had prepared what he was
going to say. 'To me, it was just one of those unfortunate
things,' he said. 'Everyone knows what that's like. It leaves
you with no way to defend yourself. Well, to me it was just
one of those unfortunate things!' He was about to continue
but the presiding judge thanked him and said that would
do. Céleste looked very upset. Then he said he wanted to
say something else. He was asked to be brief. He said once
more that it was just one of those unfortunate things. And
the presiding judge replied: 'Yes, we understand that. But

we are here precisely in order to judge this kind of unfortunate thing. Thank you.' Céleste then turned and looked at me, as if he could think of nothing else to say to show how much he wanted to help me. He looked as if he had tears in his eyes and his lips were quivering. He seemed to be silently asking me what else he could do. I said nothing, I did nothing, but for the first time in my life, I wanted to put my arms around a man. The presiding judge again asked him to step down. Céleste went and took his seat in the courtroom. He sat there for the rest of the session, leaning slightly forward, his elbows resting on his knees, holding his panama hat and listening to everything that was said.

Marie came in. She'd put on a hat and still looked beautiful. But I liked her better with her hair down. From where I was sitting, I could make out the shape of her small, shapely breasts and noticed the fullness of that lower lip I knew so well. She seemed very nervous. At once, she was asked how long she had known me. She told the court we had first met when we worked together in the same office. The presiding judge wanted to know what our relationship was. She said she was my girlfriend. In response to another question, she replied that it was true that she was going to marry me. The prosecutor leafed through his file and suddenly asked her exactly when we had started our affair. She told him. The prosecutor remarked rather casually that he seemed to recall that was a few days after Mama had died. Then he said quite sarcastically that he didn't want to dwell on such a delicate matter, that he understood Marie's scruples very well, but (and now he started sounding much harsher) that it was his duty to rise above such social niceties. So he then asked Marie to relate what had happened the day we'd first slept together. Marie didn't want to reply but the prosecutor insisted, so she said how we'd gone swimming, been to the movies and gone back to my place. The prosecutor said that after reading Marie's statement during the investigation, he had consulted the movie listings for that date. He continued, asking Marie to tell the court what film was playing that day. In an almost expressionless tone of voice, she said that, actually, it had been a Fernandel film. There was complete silence in the courtroom when she'd finished. Looking very serious, the prosecutor then stood up, and, in a tone of voice I found genuinely emotional, pointed at me and slowly began to speak: 'Gentlemen of the Jury . . . just days after his mother's death, this man went swimming, began a casual affair and went to see a comedy. I have nothing more to say.' He sat down; everyone was still silent. Then Marie suddenly burst into tears and said it wasn't like that at all, that there was more to it than that, that she was being forced to say the opposite of what she really thought, that she knew me really well and I'd done nothing wrong. But the presiding judge gestured to the clerk, who led her away and continued calling in the other witnesses.

Afterwards, they barely listened to Masson, who stated that I was an honest man 'and I'd even say, a good man'. It was the same with Salamano when he said I'd been kind to his dog and when he answered a question about my mother and me by replying that I'd had nothing more to say to Mama and that was why I'd put her in the home. 'You have to understand,' said Salamano. 'You have to understand.' But no one seemed to understand. He was led out.

Then it was Raymond's turn, the last witness. Raymond gave me a little wave and immediately said I was innocent.

But the presiding judge told him that they weren't asking his opinion, they just wanted the facts. He was politely requested to wait for the questions before replying. Then he was asked to explain his relationship with the victim. Raymond took advantage of the question to say that he was the one the dead man hated because he had slapped his sister across the face. The presiding judge asked him if the victim had any reason to hate me. Raymond replied that my presence on the beach was pure chance. The prosecutor then asked him to explain why the letter that was crucial in this matter had been written by me. Raymond replied it was a coincidence. The prosecutor retorted that coincidence had a lot to answer for in the unlawful activities at the heart of this case. He wanted to know if it was a coincidence that I hadn't intervened when Raymond slapped his mistress, a coincidence that I'd acted as a witness for him at the police station, a coincidence again that my official statement on the matter was entirely supportive of him. Finally, he asked Raymond to state his profession and when he replied: 'I work in a warehouse', the prosecutor told the jury that it was common knowledge that the witness was a pimp. I was his accomplice and his friend. This was a matter of a sordid crime of the most shameful order, worsened by the fact that it concerned a moral monster. Raymond wanted to defend himself and my lawyer objected, but they were instructed to allow the prosecutor to finish. 'I have little I wish to add,' he said, then he asked Raymond: 'Was he your friend?' 'Yes,' Raymond replied, 'he was.' The prosecutor then asked me the same question and I looked at Raymond, who was looking back at me. 'Yes,' I replied. The prosecutor then turned towards the jury and declared: 'This very man who only days after the death of his mother engaged in the most shameful, debauched behaviour, committed murder for the most petty of reasons in order to settle an unspeakably immoral dispute.'

Then he sat down. But my lawyer had had enough. Raising his arms so high that the sleeves of his gown slipped down to reveal his starched shirt, he shouted: 'Really now, I ask you, is this man on trial for having buried his mother or for having killed a man?' The spectators laughed. But the prosecutor stood up again, wrapped his robe around him and declared that only someone as naïve as the honourable defence lawyer could fail to understand how these two events were essentially, emotionally, profoundly connected. 'Yes,' he cried out, 'I accuse this man of having buried his mother with the heartlessness of a criminal.' This statement appeared to have a considerable effect on the spectators. My lawyer shrugged his shoulders and wiped away the sweat that covered his forehead. Even he seemed to be shaken up, and I realized that things weren't going well for me.

Court was adjourned. As I was led to the police car, I briefly recognized the scent and colour of a summer's evening. From the darkness of my moving prison, I rediscovered, one by one – as if arising from the depths of my weariness – all the familiar sounds of the city that I loved, and that particular moment of the day when I had sometimes felt happy. The shouts of the newspaper sellers in the calm night air, the last few birds in the town square, the people selling sandwiches, the creaking of the trams along the high bends of the city and the slight breeze from above before night suddenly falls over the port – to me, all these things merged to form the journey of a blind man, a journey I'd known so well before going to prison. Yes, this was the time of day when, a very long time ago, I had felt happy. A time when I could look forward to a night of peaceful sleep, devoid of dreams. But now, all that had changed; as I waited for the new day to dawn, I found myself back in my cell. It was as if the familiar paths etched in the summer skies could just as easily lead to prison as to innocent sleep.

# 4

Even in the dock, it is always interesting to hear people talk about you. During the summing up of the prosecutor and my defence lawyer, I can honestly say that a great deal was said about me; even more about me, perhaps, than about my crime. Were these two speeches so very different in the end? My lawyer raised his arms and pleaded guilty but with extenuating circumstances. The prosecutor stretched out his arms and denounced me as guilty but without extenuating circumstances. There was one thing, however, that upset me slightly. In spite of my anxiety, I was sometimes tempted to intervene, but my lawyer kept saying: 'The best thing you can do is to keep quiet.' It was almost as if my case was being tried without me. Everything happened without my involvement. My fate was being decided without anyone even asking my opinion. Every now and then, I had the urge to interrupt everyone and say: 'Wait a minute, who's on trial here? It's important to be the person on trial. And I have something to say!' But when I thought about it, I didn't really have anything to say. And besides, I had to admit that my desire to engage with people never lasted very long. For one thing, I quickly got bored with the prosecutor's summing up. Little snippets, certain gestures and long tirades stood out from his whole speech, but only these made an impression on me or sparked my interest.

The basis of his argument, if I understood it correctly, was that my crime was premeditated. At least that's what he tried to prove. As he himself said: 'I will provide proof of this, Gentlemen of the Jury, and in two ways. Firstly, through the blinding clarity of the facts and, secondly, through the psychological enlightenment provided to me by the sinister mind of this criminal soul.' He began by summing up the facts, starting with Mama's death. He reminded everyone of my detachment, how I hadn't known how old Mama was, how I'd gone swimming with a young woman the day after the funeral, all about the Fernandel movie and, finally, how Marie and I went home together. It took a while for me to understand what he was talking about because he kept saying 'his mistress' and, to me, she was Marie. Then he moved on to the business with Raymond. I found that his way of seeing things was actually logical; what he was saying was entirely plausible. I had written the letter with Raymond in order to tempt his mistress to return, only to be put into the hands of a man of 'dubious morality' who would treat her badly. I had goaded Raymond's enemies on the beach; Raymond had been wounded; I had asked him to give me his gun; I had gone back alone to use it; I had murdered the Arab as I had planned to. I had waited. And 'in order to make sure that the deed was properly done', I had fired four more times, deliberately, from close up, in a way that seemed more or less premeditated.

'And there you are, Gentlemen of the Jury,' said the prosecutor. 'I have explained to you the chain of events that led this man to commit murder, and with a clear understanding of his actions. And I must emphasize this point,' he said, 'for we are not dealing with an ordinary murder, an impulsive act that you might consider to be attenuated by mitigating circumstances. This man, Gentlemen of the Jury, this man is intelligent. You have heard his testimony, have you not? He knows what to say. He understands the meaning of words. And it cannot be said that he acted without knowing exactly what he was doing.'

I listened and realized I was considered intelligent. But I didn't understand how the natural qualities of an ordinary man could be turned into overwhelming proof of his guilt. At least, that was what struck me and I stopped listening to the prosecutor after that, until I heard him say: 'Did he even express any regret? Not once, Gentlemen of the Jury. Not once throughout the entire course of this investigation did this man show any remorse for his abominable crime.' He turned towards me as he said this, pointing at me as he continued his attack, and I really couldn't understand why. Of course, I had to admit he was right. I didn't really regret what I had done that much. But such viciousness astounded me. I would have liked to explain to him, politely, almost with a hint of emotion, that I have never truly been able to regret anything. I was always preoccupied by what was about to happen, either today or tomorrow. But given the position I was in, I couldn't actually speak to anyone that way. I didn't have the right to show I had feelings or good intentions. And so I tried to listen once again, because the prosecutor began talking about my soul.

He said that he had tried to look into my soul, Gentlemen of the Jury, but had failed. He said that, in truth, I had no soul, and that nothing that makes a man human, not a single moral principle, could be found within me. 'Of course,' he added, 'we should not reproach him for this. We cannot complain that he lacks what is not in his power to acquire. But where this court is concerned, tolerance, a virtue that in this instance is entirely inappropriate, must give way to the higher, more demanding virtue of justice. Especially when the lack of a soul in a man such as this becomes an abyss in which all of society can be engulfed and destroyed.' Then he started talking about my attitude towards Mama. He repeated what he'd said during the trial. But he took much longer than when he was talking about my crime, so long in fact that in the end all I could feel was the heat of that morning. At least, until the moment when the prosecutor stopped and, after a moment of silence, continued in a very low, very solemn voice: 'Tomorrow, Gentlemen of the Jury, this very court will judge the most abominable of crimes: the murder of a father.' According to him, the mind was repulsed by such a hideous act. He dared to hope that human justice would punish it without hesitation. However, and he was not afraid to say so, the horror which that crime aroused in him was almost overshadowed by the horror he felt at my cold indifference. He believed that a man who had, morally speaking, murdered his mother cut himself off from human society in the same way as someone who had actually laid a murderous hand upon the person who gave him life. In any case, the first crime paved the way for the second and, in some respects, even legitimized it. 'I am convinced, Gentlemen of the Jury,' he continued, speaking more loudly, 'that you will not find that I am exaggerating when I say that the man sitting in the dock is just as guilty of murder as the man whom this court will judge tomorrow. And he must therefore be punished for it.' The prosecutor paused to wipe the glistening sweat from his face. He said in conclusion that his duty was a painful one but that he would carry it out steadfastly. He declared that I had no place in a society whose most essential principles I disregarded and that I could not appeal for sympathy when I did not understand the heart's most basic instincts. 'I ask you for this man's head,' he said, 'and I ask for it with a clear conscience. Although there have been many times during my long career when I have been obliged to ask for the death sentence, never before have I felt this painful duty so justly counterbalanced or so strongly motivated by my awareness of a higher, sacred power and by the horror I feel when I look at the face of this man in whom I can distinguish nothing that is not monstrous.'

When the prosecutor sat down again, everyone remained silent for a long time. I was dazed by the heat and sheer astonishment. The presiding judge coughed a little and very quietly asked me if I had anything to add. I stood up and since I wanted to say something, I said, rather confusedly, that I hadn't intended to kill the Arab. The presiding judge replied that I had always made that claim but that, up until now, he had found it difficult to understand my defence and that he would be happy, before hearing my lawyer, to have me explain in detail what had motivated me to commit my crime. I said rather quickly, muddling up my words a bit and completely aware of how ridiculous I sounded, that it was because of the sun. Laughter rang out in the courtroom. My lawyer shrugged his shoulders and immediately afterwards he was given the floor. But he said that it was late, that he would need several hours for his summing up and so asked that court be adjourned until the afternoon. The presiding judge gave his consent.

That afternoon, the large fans continued to waft the heavy air around the courtroom and the jury all waved their little multi-coloured straw fans in unison. I felt as if my lawyer's summing up would never end. At one point, however, I started listening to him because he was saying: 'It is true that I killed someone.' Then he continued in the same vein, saying 'I' each time he meant me. I was very surprised. I leaned over to one of the policemen and asked why he was doing that. He told me to be quiet, but then, after a moment, he added: 'All the lawyers do it.' In my opinion, it was to distance me even further from my case, to reduce me to nothing and, in a certain way, to take my place. But I think I was already very far away from that courtroom. And besides, my lawyer seemed ridiculous. He pleaded provocation very quickly and then he too started talking about my soul. But he seemed much less skilful than the prosecutor. 'I too,' he said, 'have looked into this man's soul, but, contrary to the eminent representative of the State, I did find a soul, and I can truthfully say that to me it was an open book.' He had found that I was an honest man, a responsible employee, hard-working, loyal to my company, loved by everyone and compassionate towards other people and their problems. To him, I was a model son who had supported his mother as long as possible. In the end, I had hoped that an old people's home would give the ageing woman the kind of comfort my means would not allow me to provide for her. 'I am astounded, Gentlemen of the Jury,' he added, 'that so much importance has been placed on this home, for when all is said and done, if it were necessary to prove the usefulness and greatness of such institutions, we would be obliged to point out that it is the State itself which subsidizes them.' Only, he didn't talk about the funeral and I felt that his summing up was lacking in that respect. But because of all their long sentences, all the interminable hours and days when they had talked about my soul, I had the impression that everything was merging to form a colourless pool of swirling water that was spinning all around me.

My lawyer kept on talking and, in the end, all I really remember is the sound of an ice-cream seller's horn out in the street that resonated through the chambers of the law courts. I was overwhelmed by memories of a life that I could no longer claim as mine, a life which had offered me the most subtle but most persistent of joys: the scent of summer, the neighbourhood that I loved, a certain type of sky at night, Marie's laughter and her dresses. The sense that my presence was completely pointless here made me feel as if I were suffocating, and all I wanted was for it all to be over quickly so that I could go back to my cell and sleep. I barely heard my lawyer shouting as he concluded that the Gentlemen of the Jury would not wish to condemn to death an honest worker who had lost his head in a moment of madness, and he asked that extenuating circumstances be taken into account for a crime for which I already carried the burden of that most steadfast of punishments, eternal remorse. Court was adjourned and my lawyer sat down, looking exhausted. But his colleagues went up to him and shook his hand; I could hear them saying: 'Magnificent, sir.' One of them even asked my opinion 'Don't you think so?' he said. I agreed, but the compliment wasn't sincere because I was just too tired.

Outside, the sun was setting and the heat of the day subsiding. The occasional sounds I heard coming from the street brought with them the sweetness of the night. We were all there, waiting. And what we were all waiting for only really concerned me. I looked around the courtroom again. Everything was the same as it had been that first day. I saw the journalist in the grey jacket and the robotic little woman both looking at me. That made me realize I hadn't looked for Marie throughout the entire trial. I hadn't forgotten about her, I just had too much to do. I saw her sitting between Céleste and Raymond. She made a little gesture towards me as if to say 'Finally', and I could see she was smiling even though she looked rather nervous. But I felt my heart had hardened and I couldn't even respond to her smile.

The judges came back in. They read the members of the jury a series of questions, very quickly. I could hear 'guilty of murder' . . . 'premeditation' . . . 'extenuating circumstances'. The jury was led out and I was taken to the small room where I'd waited before. My lawyer came in to see me: he was very talkative and spoke to me with more confidence and cordiality than ever before. He thought that everything would go well and that I'd get off with a few years in prison or hard labour. I asked him if there was any chance of getting the sentence overturned if the judgement went against me. He said no. His tactic had been to file no submissions with the court so as not to antagonize the jury. He explained to me that a sentence couldn't be overturned just like that, for no reason. I found that understandable and saw his point. Looking at the matter objectively, it seemed completely natural. If it were any other way, there would be lots of paperwork for nothing. 'In any case,' my lawyer said, 'we can always appeal. But I'm convinced that we'll have a favourable outcome.'

We waited for a very long time, nearly three-quarters of an hour, I think. Then a bell rang. My lawyer said: 'The foreman of the jury will read out their decision. You'll only be called in to hear the verdict,' then he left. Doors slammed shut. People ran along staircases and I couldn't tell if they were close by or far away. Then I heard a muffled voice reading something out in the courtroom. When the bell rang again and the door of the dock was opened, the silence in the room struck me, the silence and the strange sensation I felt when I noticed that the young journalist had turned away. I didn't look over at Marie. I didn't have time to because the presiding judge told me in a strange official way that I would have my head cut off in a public place in the name of the French People. At that moment, I thought I understood the feeling I could read on all those people's faces. I believe it was a kind of respect. The policemen were very kind to me. My lawyer placed his hand on my wrist. My mind was a total blank. The presiding judge asked me if there was anything I wanted to say. I thought about it. I said: 'No.' Then I was taken away.

## 5

For the third time, I've refused to see the chaplain. I have nothing to say to him, I don't want to talk – I'll be seeing him soon enough. What I'm concerned about at present is how to avoid the guillotine, finding out if it is possible to escape the inevitable. I've been put in a different cell. When I lie down in this one, I can see the sky and nothing else. I spend all my days watching how the fading colours up above lead from day to night. Stretched out on the bed, I put my hands under my head and I wait. I don't know how many times I wondered if there were any cases of men condemned to death who managed to escape the merciless guillotine, or had vanished before their execution, or broken through the police barricade. I reproached myself for not having paid enough attention to stories about executions. People should always take an interest in those kinds of stories. You never know what might happen. I'd seen articles about executions in the papers, like everyone else. But there surely must have been special books on the subject that I was never curious enough to read. I might have found accounts of how people had managed to escape. I might have learned about one case, at least one, when the wheel of fate had stopped turning, when, just once, luck and chance had intervened to halt that powerful driving force. Just once! In a way, I think that would have been enough. My heart would have done the rest. The newspapers often talk about a debt that is owed to society. And that debt has to be paid, they say. But that doesn't really fire the imagination. What counted was the possibility of escape, a leap beyond the merciless rite, a rush towards the kind of madness that offered every possibility of hope. Of course, all you could hope for was to be shot down by some stray bullet as you turned a corner while running away as fast as you could. But, all things considered, nothing allowed me such a luxury, everything conspired against me, the guillotine was going to have me.

In spite of my willingness to accept this glaring certainty, I simply couldn't. Because, in reality, from the moment judgement was passed, the evidence my sentence was based on seemed ridiculously out of proportion to its inevitable conclusion. The fact that the sentence had been read out at eight o'clock in the evening rather than at five o'clock, that it might have been completely different, that it had been decided by ordinary men, that it had been proclaimed in the name of a concept as vague as the French (or German or Chinese) People, all these things seemed to prove that such a judgement had not been made conscientiously. And yet, I had no choice but to admit that from the moment sentence was passed, its impact became as certain, as real, as the solid wall of my cell against which I pressed my body.

At moments like these, I would remember a story my mother had told me that concerned my father. I never knew him. All I knew for sure about the man was what my mother told me about him: he had gone to see a murderer being executed. He was sick at the thought of going. He had gone nonetheless and when he got home, he had thrown up for part of the morning. This story about my father disgusted me a little back then. Now, I understood; it was so natural. How could I have not realized that nothing is more important than an execution and that, all in all, it was the only thing of real interest to a man! If I ever got out of this prison, I would go to see every single public execution. I was wrong, I think, to consider that possibility. Because whenever I imagined myself free one day, at dawn, behind a police cordon, on the other side of it, so to speak, as a spectator who had come to watch and could then go home and be sick, a wave of bitter joy spread through my heart. But even admitting the possibility wasn't sensible. I was wrong to let myself get carried away by such thoughts because a second later I would feel so horribly cold that I would have to huddle up under my blanket. My teeth would start chattering and there was nothing I could do to stop it.

But naturally, it's impossible to be logical all the time. For example, sometimes I would dream up new laws. I would reform the penal code. I had noticed that the most important thing was to give the condemned man a chance. One chance in a thousand; even that would be enough to put things right. It seemed to me that it should be possible to find a chemical compound that would kill the patient (that's what I thought: the patient) nine times out of ten. The patient would be told; that would be a condition. Because after giving it a lot of thought, after considering things calmly, I understood what was flawed about the guillotine: no one had a chance, none whatsoever. When all was said and done, the death of the patient had been decided, once and for all. The matter was closed; it was an immutable mechanism, a foregone conclusion, not open for discussion. If by some extraordinary chance anything went wrong, they would simply start all over again. And so, logically, what was really annoying was that the condemned man had to hope for the guillotine to function properly. This is where I'd say the system is definitely faulty. And it's true in a way. Yet I had to admit that this system held the secret of good management. Because, when all was said and done, the condemned man was obliged to collaborate morally: it was in his own best interest that everything went smoothly.

I also had to admit that up until now I'd had ideas on this matter that weren't really correct. For a long time, I had believed – though I don't know why – that to reach the guillotine, you had to walk up some steps to the scaffold. I think it was because of the 1789 Revolution; I mean because of everything I'd been taught or shown about it. But one morning, I remembered a photograph I'd seen published in the newspapers about a sensational execution. The guillotine had actually been set down on the ground, as simply as that. It was much narrower than I'd imagined. I hadn't realized this before, which was rather odd. I had been struck by how well constructed it looked in the picture: precision-made, polished and gleaming. People always have exaggerated ideas about unfamiliar things. I had to admit though that, in this case, everything was very simple: the guillotine was positioned at the same level as the man walking towards it. He walked over to it as if he were going to meet someone. That was also annoying. The imagination could connect with the idea of walking up the steps to the scaffold, ascending to the open skies. But the guillotine killed even that idea: you were executed discreetly, with a bit of shame and a great deal of precision.

There were two other things I thought about all the time: the coming of dawn and my appeal. But I tried to be logical and stop thinking about them. I would stretch out, look up at the sky and force myself to find it interesting. It was turning a greenish colour: it was evening. I made another effort to think about something else. I listened to my heart beating. I simply couldn't believe that this sound that had been with me for so long would ever end. I've never had any real imagination. But I did try to imagine the very moment when I would no longer hear the beating of my heart. In vain. The dawn and my appeal were still there. I ended up telling myself that it made sense not to fight it.

They'd come for me at dawn, I knew that much. In fact, I spent all my nights waiting for that dawn. I've never liked surprises. When something is going to happen to me, I prefer to know about it. That's why I ended up sleeping only for a short time during the day, and all through the night I patiently waited for the morning light to slip slowly from the sky through my window. The most difficult time was the frightening moment when I knew they normally come for you. After midnight, I watched and waited. Never had I heard so many different noises, so many distant sounds. But I can honestly say that throughout that entire time I was lucky, because I never heard the sound of footsteps. Mama often said that no one is ever really entirely unhappy. I agreed with her here in my prison, when the sky took on so many colours and the light of a new day gradually flowed into my cell. Because I might have heard footsteps and my heart might have burst. Even though the slightest sound of something slipping past my door made me rush over to it, even though I waited, horrified, my ear pressed against the wood, until I could hear my own breathing again, terrified to hear it sounding so hoarse and so like a dog in its death throes, when all was said and done, my heart did not burst and, once more, I'd won another twenty-four hours.

All day long, I thought of my appeal. I believe I got the most I could out of this idea. I calculated my chances and exploited such thinking to the full. I always assumed the worst: my appeal would be denied. 'Well then, I'll die.' Sooner than other people, that much was obvious. But everyone knows that life isn't really worth living. In the end, I knew that it didn't matter much whether you died at thirty or at seventy, because in either case other men and women would of course go on living, and it would be like that for thousands of years. Nothing was more obvious, in fact. But I was still the one who would be dying, whether it was now or in twenty years. When I thought about that, though, what truly upset me was the horrible lurch I felt inside at the thought of twenty years of life yet to live. But all I had to do to banish that feeling was to imagine what my thoughts would be like twenty years from now when I would have to face the same situation. If you are going to die, it didn't actually matter how or when, that much was obvious. And so (and what was really difficult was not losing sight of everything that this 'and so' symbolized in my thinking), and so, I had to accept that my appeal would be denied.

At that point, and only at that point, I had the right, so to speak, to allow myself to entertain the notion of the second possibility: I would be pardoned. What was annoying, how-ever, was that I then had to control the fiery rush of blood through my body that burned my eyes with unimaginable joy. I had to concentrate in order to be logical, to silence that piercing call from deep within me. I had to remain calm at the thought of this possibility in order to make my resignation in the face of the first assumption more believ-able. When I succeeded, I earned an hour of peace. And that, to tell the truth, was a considerable feat.

It was at just such a moment that I again refused to see the chaplain. I was stretched out on my bed and I could tell that the summer's evening was fast approaching because the sky took on a certain golden colour. I had just dismissed the idea of winning my appeal and I could feel the blood flowing through me in calm waves. I didn't need to see the chaplain. For the first time in a very long while, I thought about Marie. She had stopped writing to me a long time ago. That evening, I considered the situation and decided she had perhaps grown tired of being the mistress of a man condemned to death. It also occurred to me that she might be sick or dead. Such things happen; it was natural. There was no way of knowing because apart from our two bodies, now separated, nothing bound us to each other, nothing kept us alive to each other. Although, if I discovered that was the case, I would become indifferent to the memory of Marie. She would no longer interest me once she was dead. I found that idea normal, just as I completely understood why people would forget me after I died. They would no longer have anything to do with me. I couldn't even say that such an idea was difficult to accept.

It was at precisely that moment that the chaplain arrived.

When I saw him, I started shaking a little. He noticed and told me not to be afraid. I said that he usually came at a different time of day. He replied that he was making a friendly visit and it had nothing to do with my appeal; he knew nothing about that. He sat down on my bed and asked me to sit next to him. I said no. He seemed very kind, though.

He remained seated there for a moment, his forearms resting on his knees, head lowered, looking at his hands. They were slim, muscular hands; they reminded me of two supple animals. He slowly rubbed them against each other. He simply sat there, head still lowered, for such a long time that I had the impression, just for a moment, that I'd forgotten he was there.

But he suddenly raised his head and looked straight at me. 'Why,' he asked, 'why have you refused to see me?' I replied that I didn't believe in God. He wanted to know if I was absolutely sure of that and I told him it was not something I needed to question: it seemed a matter of no importance. He then leaned back against the wall, resting his hands against his thighs. Almost without seeming to be speaking to me, he remarked that people sometimes thought they were sure when, in reality, they weren't. I said nothing. He looked at me and asked: 'What do you think about that idea?' I replied that it was possible. In any case, even if I wasn't sure about what truly interested me, I was absolutely sure about what didn't interest me. And what he was talking about definitely didn't interest me.

He looked away and, staying very still, asked me if I was talking this way because I was in terrible despair. I explained that I wasn't in despair. I was just afraid, which was completely natural. 'God could help you, then,' he said. 'Everyone

I have known in your position has come back to Him.' I agreed that was their right. It also proved they had time on their side. As far as I was concerned, though, I didn't want anyone's help and, more to the point, I didn't have time to waste thinking about things that didn't interest me.

He threw up his hands in frustration, then stood up and rearranged the folds of his robe. When he'd finished, he started talking to me, calling me 'my friend': if he spoke to me this way, it wasn't because I was condemned to death; in his opinion, we were all condemned to death. But I cut in and said it wasn't the same thing and, besides, that wasn't any consolation. 'Of course,' he agreed, 'but you will still die at some point even if it's not today. You will have to face the same situation. How will you deal with this terrible trial?' I replied that I'd deal with it exactly as I was dealing with it now.

He stood up after I'd said that and looked straight at me. It was a game I knew very well. I often used to amuse myself by playing it with Emmanuel or Céleste and, usually, they were the ones who looked away first. The chaplain also knew this game very well. I realized that immediately: he didn't waver. And his voice didn't falter either when he said: 'Have you no hope whatsoever? Do you really live with the belief that there is nothing after death?' 'Yes,' I replied.

He lowered his head and sat down again. He told me he felt sorry for me. He thought it would be unbearable for anyone to live with such a belief. But all I felt was that he was beginning to bore me. I turned away and stood beneath the window. I leaned against the wall. Without really following what he was saying, I heard him start questioning me again; his voice was anxious and insistent. I realized he was trembling with emotion, so I started listening to him more carefully.

He told me he was sure that my appeal would be granted but I was carrying a heavy sin and I had to unburden myself. According to him, the justice of man was nothing, and the justice of God, everything. I pointed out that it was the former that had condemned me. He replied that, nevertheless, it had not cleansed my sin. I said I didn't know what sin meant. I'd only been told I was guilty. I was guilty, I was paying for it, no one could ask any more of me. He stood up then and I thought that if he wanted to move at all in this very narrow cell, he had no choice. You either had to sit down or stand up.

I was staring down at the ground. He took a step towards me then stopped, as if he were afraid to come any closer. He looked up at the sky through the bars on the window. 'You're mistaken, my son,' he said. 'More could be asked of you. Perhaps it will be asked of you.' 'What do you mean?' 'You could be asked to see.' 'To see what?'

The priest looked all around him and spoke in a voice that seemed suddenly very weary: 'Pain and sadness are seeping out of all these stones, I know that. I've never looked at them without feeling anguish. But deep within my heart, I know that even the most despondent of men has seen a divine face emerge from the darkness, and it is that face I am asking you to see.'

I reacted to that a bit. I said I'd been staring at these walls for months. There was nothing and no one I knew better in the world. Perhaps, a long time ago, I'd tried to see a face emerge from these walls. But that face glowed with the colour of the sun and the flame of desire: it was Marie's face.

I'd looked for it in vain. Now, all that was over. And in any case, I'd never seen anything emerge from these glistening walls.

The priest looked at me with a kind of sadness. I was now leaning flat against the wall, my face bathed in sunlight. He said a few words I didn't hear, then asked me very quickly if I'd let him embrace me. 'No,' I replied. He turned around and walked over to the wall, slowly feeling it with his hand: 'Do you love this world so much, then?' he murmured. I didn't reply.

For a long time, he stood there with his back to me. His presence weighed heavily on me, irritated me. I was about to tell him to go, to leave me alone, when he suddenly turned towards me and shouted passionately: 'No, I cannot believe you. I am sure you have sometimes wished for another life.' I replied that of course I had, but I might just as well have wished to be rich, or to swim very fast or to have a more beautifully shaped mouth. It was of the same order. But he broke in and wanted to know how I imagined this other life. So I shouted: 'A life that would remind me of this one,' and without stopping, I told him I'd had enough. He wanted to talk to me about God a little longer, but I walked over to him and tried to explain once and for all that I had very little time left and I didn't want to waste it on God. He tried to change the subject by asking me why I called him 'Sir' instead of 'Father'. That annoyed me and I told him he wasn't my father: he might be to other people.

'No, my son,' he said, putting his hand on my shoulder. I am here for you. But you cannot understand that because your heart is blind. I will pray for you.'

Then, I don't know why, something burst inside me.

I started shouting at the top of my lungs and swore at him and told him not to pray for me. I grabbed him by the collar of his cassock. I poured out all the feelings that surged up from the depths of my heart in waves of anger and joy. He seemed so sure of himself, didn't he? But not one of his certainties was worth a single strand of a woman's hair. He wasn't even sure he was alive because he lived life as if he were dead. I may look as if I had nothing but I was sure of myself, sure of everything, sure of my life, sure of my impending death. Yes, that was all I had. But at least I had a hold on that truth as much as it had a hold on me. I'd been right, I was still right, I had always been right. I had lived my life a certain way when I could have lived it another way. I had done one thing when I might have done something else. What difference did it make? I felt as if I had been waiting all this time for this very moment and this early dawn when I would be vindicated. Nothing, *nothing* mattered and I knew very well why. He also knew why. From the depths of my future, throughout all this absurd life I had lived, a gathering wind swept towards me, stripping bare along its path everything that had been possible in the years gone by, years that seemed just as unreal as the ones that lay ahead. Why should the death of other people or a mother's love matter so much? Why should I care about his god, the lives, the destinies we choose when one unique destiny had chosen me, and along with me millions and millions of privileged others who, like him, called themselves my brothers? Couldn't he understand, could he really not understand? Everyone was privileged. There was no one who wasn't privileged. All those others, they too would one day be condemned to death. He as well, he too would be condemned to death. What did it matter if accused of murder he was executed for not crying at his mother's funeral? Salamano's dog was as important as his wife. The little robotic lady was just as guilty as the Parisian woman Masson had married, just as guilty as Marie, who wanted me to marry her. What difference did it make if Raymond was my friend as well as Céleste, who was a better person than him? What did it matter if Marie was now offering her lips to a new Meursault? Couldn't this condemned man understand, and from the depths of my future ... I was choking as I shouted all this. The guards had already pulled the priest from my grasp and were threatening me. But he calmed them down and looked at me for a moment in silence. His eyes were full of tears. He turned around and walked out.

After he'd gone, I calmed down again. I was exhausted and threw myself down on the bed. I think I fell asleep because when I woke up, the stars were shining on my face. The sounds of the countryside drifted towards me. The scent of the night, the earth and the salt air cooled my temples. The wonderful peacefulness of this sleepy summer flowed through me in great waves. At that moment, just as day was dawning, I heard the wail of sirens. They announced a journey to a world that was forever indifferent to my fate. For the first time in a very long while, I thought about Mama. I believed I understood why at the end of her life she had taken a 'fiancé', why she had taken the chance to start over again. There at the home, where lives faded away, there as well, evening offered a wistful moment of peace. So close to death, Mama must have felt set free, ready to live once more. No one – *no one* – had the right to cry over her. And I as well, I too felt ready to start life all over again. As if this great release of anger had purged me of evil, emptied me of hope; and standing before this symbolic night bursting with stars, I opened myself for the first time to the tender indifference of the world. To feel it so like me, so like a brother, in fact, I understood that I had been happy, and I was still happy. So that it might be finished, so that I might feel less alone, I could only hope there would be many, many spectators on the day of my execution and that they would greet me with cries of hatred.

# THE FALL

## *Albert Camus*

'Because I desired eternal life, I slept with whores and drank for whole nights on end'

Jean-Baptiste Clamence is a soul in turmoil. Over several drunken nights he regales a chance acquaintance with his story. From this successful former lawyer and seemingly model citizen a compelling, self-loathing catalogue of guilt, hypocrisy and alienation pours forth.

*The Fall* is a brilliant portrayal of a man who has glimpsed the hollowness of his existence. But beyond depicting one man's disillusionment, Camus's novel exposes the universal human condition and its absurdities – and our innocence that, once lost, can never be recaptured . . .

'An irresistibly brilliant examination of modern conscience' *The New York Times*

# THE PLAGUE

## *Albert Camus*

'This empty town, white with dust, saturated with sea smells, loud with the howl of the wind'

The townspeople of Oran are in the grip of a deadly plague, which condemns its victims to a swift and horrifying death. Fear, isolation and claustrophobia follow as they are forced into quarantine. Each person responds in their own way to the lethal disease: some resign themselves to fate, some seek blame, and a few, like Dr Rieux, resist the terror.

An immediate triumph when it was published in 1947, The Plague is in part an allegory of France's suffering under the Nazi occupation, and a story of bravery and determination against the precariousness of human existence.

'Enduring fiction has the power to grow into new kinds of timeliness' Boyd Tonkin, *Independent*

# A HAPPY DEATH

*Albert Camus*

Is it possible to die a happy death? This is the question at the heart of Camus' astonishing early novel. It tells the story of the choices that face a young Algerian who defies society's rules by committing a murder and escaping punishment, and then experiments with different ways of life on his journey towards a death 'without anger, without hatred, without regret'.

Published posthumously, *A Happy Death* is in many ways a fascinating first sketch for *The Outsider,* but it can also be seen as a candid self-portrait, drawing on Camus' youth, travels and early relationships to create a lyrical, dreamlike picture of the sun-drenched Algiers of his childhood.

'One of the most eloquent existentialist voices' *The Times*

# CALIGULA AND OTHER PLAYS

## *Albert Camus*

Camus' powerful drama 'Caligula' portrays a monstrous, nihilistic Emperor who, in destroying everything around him, ultimately destroys men, gods and even himself. The other philosophical plays collected here also reveal his deep sense of the human condition: 'Cross Purpose', which show a universe in which cruel, inexplicable things happen to innocent and evil alike, and the more overtly political works 'The Just' and 'The Possessed', which dramatize action and revolt in the name of liberty, and question whether violence can ever be justified. Taken together, these plays illustrate a shift in Camus' perceptions: from the existentialist perception of life's absurdity to a more humane, politically engaged world view.

'Few French writers have been more versatile or more influential than Camus' *The Times*

# DUBLINERS

## *James Joyce*

James Joyce's *Dubliners* is an enthralling collection of modernist short stories which create a vivid picture of the day-to-day experience of Dublin life. This Penguin Classics edition includes notes and an introduction by Terence Brown.

Joyce's first major work, written when he was only twenty-five, brought his city to the world for the first time. His stories are rooted in the rich detail of Dublin life, portraying ordinary, often defeated lives with unflinching realism. From 'The Sisters', a vivid portrait of childhood faith and guilt, to 'Araby', a timeless evocation of the inexplicable yearnings of adolescence, to 'The Dead', in which Gabriel Conroy is gradually brought to a painful epiphany regarding the nature of his existence, Joyce draws a realistic and memorable cast of Dubliners together in an powerful exploration of overarching themes. Writing of social decline, sexual desire and exploitation, corruption and personal failure, he creates a brilliantly compelling, unique vision of the world and of human experience.

'Joyce celebrates the lives of ordinary men and women' Anthony Burgess, *Observer*

# BONJOUR TRISTESSE AND A CERTAIN SMILE

*Françoise Sagan*

Published when she was only eighteen, Françoise Sagan's astonishing first novel *Bonjour Tristesse* became an instant bestseller. It tells the story of Cécile, who leads a carefree life with her widowed father and his young mistresses until, one hot summer on the Riviera, he decides to remarry – with devastating consequences. In *A Certain Smile* Dominique, a young woman bored with her lover, begins an encounter with an older man that unfolds in unexpected and troubling ways.

These stylish, shimmering and amoral tales had explicit sexual scenes removed for English publication in the 1950s. Now this fresh and accurate new translation presents the uncensored text of Sagan's masterpieces in full for the first time.

'Funny, thoroughly immoral and thoroughly French' *The Times*

## LOLITA

*Vladimir Nabokov*

'Lolita, light of my life, fire of my loins. My sin, my soul.'

Humbert Humbert – scholar, aesthete and romantic – has fallen completely and utterly in love with Lolita Haze, his landlady's gum-snapping, silky skinned twelve-year-old daughter. Reluctantly agreeing to marry Mrs Haze just to be close to Lolita, Humbert suffers greatly in the pursuit of romance; but when Lo herself starts looking for attention elsewhere, he will carry her off on a desperate cross-country misadventure, all in the name of Love. Hilarious, flamboyant, heart-breaking and full of ingenious word play, *Lolita* is an immaculate, unforgettable masterpiece of obsession, delusion and lust.

'There's no funnier monster in modern literature than poor, doomed Humbert Humbert' *Independent*

# METAMORPHOSIS AND OTHER STORIES

*Franz Kafka*

'When Gregor Samsa awoke one morning from troubled dreams, he found himself changed into a monstrous cockroach in his bed'

Kafka's masterpiece of unease and black humour, *Metamorphosis*, the story of an ordinary man transformed into an insect, is brought together in this collection with the rest of his works that he thought worthy of publication. It includes *Meditation*, a collection of his earlier studies; *The Judgement*, written in a single night of frenzied creativity; 'The Stoker', the first chapter of a novel set in America; and a fascinating occasional piece, 'The Aeroplanes at Brescia', Kafka's eyewitness account of an air display in 1909. Together, these stories reveal the breadth of his literary vision and the extraordinary imaginative depth of his thought.

'What Dante and Shakespeare were for the ages, Kafka is for ours'
George Steiner